"Intelligent, spooky, original, and fall-down funny, ~~~ ~~~ layers from page one."—JASON EMDE, AUTHOR OF *LITTLE BIT DIE*

"Robyn Braun's *The Head* pulses with the abject horror of those worrying parts of your being you can't put your finger on but just can't seem to throw away."—K.I. PRESS AUTHOR OF *EXQUISITE MONSTERS, TYPES OF CANADIAN WOMEN, SPINE,* AND *PALE RED FOOTPRINTS*

"A stunning achievement: compelling, disturbing, and thought-provoking, the sort of book that stays with you long after you finish it."—MICHELLE BARKER, AUTHOR OF *MY LONG LIST OF IMPOSSIBLE THINGS,* AND *THE HOUSE OF 1000 EYES*

"Astonishing and smart. *The Head* will leave you thinking long after the last word."—ROBIN VAN ECK, AUTHOR OF *ROUGH*

"*The Head* is sharp, funny, compelling and profound. Taut as a guitar string. A wonderful debut from a writer to watch."—SABYASACHI NAG, AUTHOR OF *HANDS LIKE TREES*

"Propulsive and darkly comedic, *The Head*, takes a good honest look at what it means to carry childhood trauma into adulthood. A whirlwind read that will make you laugh, cry, grit your teeth, and ultimately, feel at peace. Highly recommend! "—SHELLY KAWAJA, AUTHOR OF *THE RAW LIGHT OF MORNING*

"Robyn Braun's *The Head*, is a strange, terrifying novella that reminds me of Kafka and Amparo Davila, with flashes of Yoko Ogawa. This allegoric story about a woman who shuffles back and forth across the intensely patriarchal worlds of family and academia, is told with spare strokes and macabre detail, showcasing a disturbing vision for the narrow lives of the people trapped within them. Braun unflinchingly explores the dark side of an intellectually demanding career, love, and the desire for independence, and delivers an ending that will haunt readers long after the final line."—JOHN VIGNA, AUTHOR OF *NO MAN'S LAND*

"On her thirtieth birthday, Trish hears a cry in the shower and emerges to find a tiny disembodied head. Soggy, weeping, squishy, moist, the head is everything least acceptable to the hallowed halls of the STEM research institution where Trish seeks tenure. Failed on all sides by lovers, colleagues, students, counselors, and supervisors who seem unable to differentiate between a thing Trish has done and a thing that has happened to her, Trish travels back to her parents and her past in search of answers. Reminiscent of Carmen Maria Machado's unsettling speculative explorations of female pain, Robyn Braun's *The Head* is eerie, fiercely embodied, and darkly hilarious. What do we do with shame, Braun asks, when we can't carry it and we don't know how to set it down?"
—BRONWEN TATE, AUTHOR OF *THE SILK THE MOTHS IGNORE*

Enfield & Wizenty (an imprint of Great Plains Publications)
320 Rosedale Ave
Winnipeg, MB R3L 1L8
www.greatplains.mb.ca

Great Plains Publications gratefully acknowledges the financial support provided for its publishing program by the Government of Canada through the Canada Book Fund; the Canada Council for the Arts; the Province of Manitoba through the Book Publishing Tax Credit and the Book Publisher Marketing Assistance Program; and the Manitoba Arts Council.

Design & Typography by Relish New Brand Experience
Printed in Canada by Friesens

Library and Archives Canada Cataloguing in Publication

Title: The head / Robyn Braun.
Names: Braun, Robyn, author.
Identifiers: Canadiana 20240290135 | ISBN 9781773371153 (softcover)
Subjects: LCGFT: Novels.
Classification: LCC PS8603.R3832 H43 2024 | DDC C813/.6—dc23

ENVIRONMENTAL BENEFITS STATEMENT

Great Plains Press saved the following resources by printing the pages of this book on chlorine free paper made with 100% post-consumer waste.

TREES	WATER	ENERGY	SOLID WASTE	GREENHOUSE GASES
3	**260**	**1**	**12**	**1,440**
FULLY GROWN	GALLONS	MILLION BTUs	POUNDS	POUNDS

Environmental impact estimates were made using the Environmental Paper Network Paper Calculator 4.0. For more information visit www.papercalculator.org

Canadä

FSC
www.fsc.org
MIX
Paper | Supporting responsible forestry
FSC® C016245

THE HEAD

ROBYN BRAUN

ENFIELD
&WIZENTY

CHAPTER ONE

At least the faculty meeting was in the afternoon; Trish had time to institute her new routine. It was her birthday—thirty—and she was determined to move through the world in a different manner. She couldn't decide on the right word. Composure, grace, equanimity? The exact word didn't matter. It would feel smooth and sleek. Like satin. At thirty, she would allow for only satin-like comportment. This morning, for example, instead of dozing while her coffee perked, she hopped into the shower. This was a better use of time; more appropriate to a composed thirty-year-old. The headaches would not persist once the routine was established. Maybe she would even drink less coffee.

At the far end of the tub, Trish shielded herself from the spray, chiding her weak will. Such a waste of water. Besides, some bearded Dutch guy was all over the internet telling people that cold water's good for you. Holding her breath, she forced the back of her neck under the spray.

And that's when the cry rang out. She peered out the shower curtain, but all was still. Now the water was warm. Letting the conditioner soak into her hair, she soaped her pits. The cry came again. It couldn't be a cry. Maybe the pipes? It was an older building and occasionally the pipes shrilled. But that sound typically came with a juddering that shook the building. The cry again. But this time it had a little cough at the end.

Maybe the perk was boiling over. Lost coffee. Of course, she could not pull off the new routine. She poked her head out of the shower again to listen but could not hear the tell-tale hiss of coffee hitting the hot burner. The sound was very wet. Almost like choking.

She stared at the bottom of the tub, listening. Water spread around her feet and slipped down the drain. The slimy pipe, with its layers of dead skin cells and mould. Green-black strata coming away in hunks. Trish gagged. The word gelatinous stuck in her head. Gelatinous. She stood farther from the drain and rinsed her hair as quickly as possible.

Out of the shower, the sound persisted. At least it wasn't the drain. Gelatinous. She wrapped a towel around herself and ran on her toes to the kitchen. Brown water bubbled happily into the perk's glass cap. She poured herself a cup, blew and sipped, and closed her eyes in pleasure as the liquid scalded her throat.

The sound came again, sharper this time. From down the hall. Maybe Anne's drain upstairs was plugged. The building was usually pristine with quiet. Noise had been a major talking point with the landlord when Trish rented the apartment.

"It's an adults-only building," he said. "Kids make too much noise."

Trish was pretty sure it was some kind of human rights violation not to allow children to live somewhere. Like saying a building was for MENSA members only, or no left-handed people allowed. What did a person's development have to do with where they were allowed to live? Surely nothing?

"Adults can be noisy too," Trish countered.

"Not here, they can't."

She did not love the man's frontier attitude, but she did like quiet, and he said he didn't come around much. He relegated the tasks of managing the building to Trish's downstairs neighbour, Ken, who got a break in his rent for the work he did around the building. Ken played guitar in a local band.

"What about the noise?" Trish was sure she had a point. Why was she arguing?

But the landlord waved away her question. "It's acoustic."

And she never did hear Ken practice, only ever saw him put a guitar case in his hatchback and drive off in the late evening. The band was Ken's only employment. He spent afternoons smoking pot in the back garden, which was supposed to be shared. But Trish didn't garden.

When would Ken be awake to deal with whatever was causing the noise? She took a sip from her mug so it wouldn't spill as she walked, and turned toward the sound, which she could hear now was coming from down the hall. It was a damp sound, but occasionally sharp. Viscous. Gelatinous. The snap of gluey liquid. Maybe Anne was having work done on her radiators.

As Trish turned into the doorframe of her bedroom, the question of the sound resolved itself into an entirely new set of problems. On top of her dresser quivered a mass of fleshy pink sludge, slurping and snapping. Cold horror shot through the back of her neck and across her shoulders, freezing the breath at the bottom of her throat.

The thing was not enormous. Fairly small, in fact. She could have held it in one hand. The size of a doll's head, a grapefruit. But alive. Vital. Emitting sound as a function of its existence. Gripping the towel tightly across her chest, she bent slowly and placed the coffee on her nightstand. Then she backed out of the doorway. The thing on the dresser wailed.

Trish fled. Ran. Straight back down the hall into the bathroom. She pushed herself against the window in the corner between the tub and the sink, grabbed the shower curtain and pulled it across her body, right up to her nose, wedging a leg in behind the tub, the sharp rim pressing into her thigh. She watched the door and listened hard for the sound of the floor creaking. Nothing moved. There was no sound. The apartment was perfectly still. When she was sure of the silence, she dropped the shower curtain and pulled her thigh out from behind the tub and stood listening. Silence. She stepped toward the sink. What was happening? Behind her the shower curtain moved, and she snapped around to face it. But it was just settling back into place. Silence settled again.

At the sink she cupped her hands and drank from the cold faucet. Then she stared into her own eyes in the mirror. What had she done? What brought this terror into her bedroom? It wasn't like she'd had anything to drink the night before. So pathetic was her social life—the night before her thirtieth birthday and she was asleep before eleven. Was she *still* asleep? Was she hallucinating even her reflection in the mirror? Was her mind playing tricks on her? Was the stress of work causing her to see things? Hear things? Another howl came from her room. A net of electricity hummed under her skin. She reached over and closed the bathroom door. The sound dimmed. Surely if the noise was in her head, it would not have done so.

The movement of closing the door made Trish slightly dizzy. She sat on the toilet. What was that thing? How had it arrived? Had someone been in the apartment and left it there while she showered? The landlord? Who had a key? Why would the landlord do that to her? Maybe it had been delivered on behalf of someone. What had she done to deserve it?

In her mind's eye, her father shook his head in silent incredulity. Her stomach hurt and sweat pooled in the folds of her belly. She sat up straight, easing the pressure on her guts and took a deep breath. He was not here. He had no knowledge of what was happening.

Her back tickled and she pulled her shoulder blades together. Be sensible. For one thing, she needed to get dressed. Dealing with this thing at all would require that she be dressed. Besides, her coffee was in there, which she also needed. The thing could not get up to hurt her. It had no legs or appendages. It would lie there on the dresser, making sticky sounds. She could pull the drawers open and get clothes, gather everything up and run back here to the bathroom. Maybe upon second glance the thing would not be a horror but would have an explanation. She stood up and blew out a sharp breath, like she was going to run a race. Tiptoeing down the hall, she trailed her fingers along the wall's cool, pitted plaster, and then peered through the bedroom doorway. The fleshy lump was not crying at the moment, only emanating nasty smacks and burbles. Long slow steps brought her quietly to the bedside table, where she seized her coffee.

She tightened her stomach muscles and approached the dresser slowly, stopping completely before each new foray forward, keeping a very close eye on the moving mass. As she got closer, Trish saw that the thing was not just a mass of flesh. There were points of differentiation. And finally, when she was one step away from the dresser, she saw.

It was a head. A fully formed, miniature head. Not the wizened, old, shrunken heads from those books of *strange, but true facts*. The thing was fleshy, blood-filled, mobile. Terrified and resistant, Trish took one more step closer so she could peer down over the thing. There was no wound where its neck should be; the skin under the chin was mostly smooth, with small puckers at its very edge. If the head had been cut and sewn, that would mean someone had handled it. Its skin was pale like Trish's and the entire thing was a splotchy red. All that crying. Its eyes were a deep but clear blue that Trish had never seen.

She shook her head like a dog will shake its head as it backs away from porcupine quills stuck in its snout, and lowered herself to the edge of the bed, staring at the thing on her dresser. It looked like a little baby head. Trish turned quickly and pulled the blanket back from the bed, searching for blood. Had she birthed the thing? There was no blood. She seized her pyjama pants from the floor. Unmarked. With two fingers, she spread her labia and felt up into her vagina thinking, even as she did it, she didn't know what she was feeling for. But her vagina felt exactly as it always did. And her fingers came out clean and shiny. Trish was unsure if she was relieved or not.

Where had this thing come from? Trish checked the ceiling. Intact. But the thought of the thing passing through the plane of the ceiling made her consider the possibility of perspective. It was possible she didn't have the right perspective on the thing. She stood and stepped to the end of the dresser, and then peered directly along its surface to the head. The little face ballooned out at her as though she had placed a magnifying glass in front of it. Trish recoiled. She had one last idea. Keeping her hand below the dresser's edge, she reached around and pulled open the top drawer, and then squatted low to inspect the underside of the spot where the head rested. Nothing. The head smacked its lips loudly. If the thing required another perspective, it would need time to unfold. Trish had to deal with it for now.

Did someone hate her? Enough to desire this fear for her? Enough to have this thing put upon her—arrange for its arrival. Who had access to such grotesquerie? Ought she to call someone? Not an ambulance. The thing did not appear to need medical attention. And imagine what the paramedics would think. And if they took the head, the doctors at the hospital would have similar thoughts. How would Trish handle that?

"I know you're *usually* the smartest people in the room …"

Besides, medicine could answer no question with respect to its arrival. It wasn't part of a living system about which medicine was already familiar. It had to be of a system though. Perhaps it was only the shadow of a system. Maybe it was a matter for science though, and she was being irresponsible. Maybe she should contact some authority? The police? In fact, maybe someone had broken in. Trish imagined showing uniformed police into her room and gesturing to the thing on the dresser. No. She could not bear their questions. And what if they somehow thought she was responsible? What if, once alerted, the authorities saw this was Trish's fault? If they took her in, arrested her, she would need help, which would mean her parents. How would she explain the head to them? Best to handle it on her own. For now, at least.

She wanted to call Luca. Her phone had a birthday message from Jess. Immediately her despair deepened. Her birthday composure had not lasted for even an hour. And such a colossal loss of control too. What could she possibly say to Jess? It was going to have to wait. She opened drawers slowly and pulled out clothes, never taking her eyes off the head, and then backed out of the room, clothes and phone clutched to her chest. On the dresser, the head cried. Trish's heartbeat shook her hands.

In the bathroom, she dialled Luca's number. Luca had been Trish's lover for a couple of years, and she knew he loved her. But he had recently called off the affair because his wife wanted a divorce. Trish thought that should free him up, but he said the divorce was exhausting and he didn't have the energy for their relationship.

She set the ringing phone on the edge of the sink and maneuvered into her bra. Luca's phone rang and rang. Of course. He wouldn't answer it. Not the first time. She pulled her shirt over her head. When the robot voice told her the customer at this number was not available, she hung up and finished pulling on her jeans. Then she dialled again. And again. She paced the bathroom and took sips of coffee as the phone rang. After four tries, she knew he wouldn't pick up. A text.

> Where are you? I need you.

Waiting for the jumping bubbles, she continued to pace the bathroom. Luca wasn't teaching. And it was too early for him to be at the gym. Why wasn't he answering? Maybe he had a meeting and had left his phone in his office. Maybe he had gone down to the coffee machine, or the washroom. She couldn't wait. She had to do something now—get out. Maybe if she left the apartment, her head would clear and when she came back, that thing would be gone. It had arrived without her awareness. Maybe it would only leave when she wasn't aware. She texted him.

> I really need you.
> Meet me at Dabster's.
> Please.

Dabster's was a coffee shop halfway between the university and Trish's place. Far enough from Luca's house that he was comfortable meeting there.

The thing was still wailing down the hall. She was not going to walk past it. She would go out through the kitchen door and down the back steps from the balcony. A pair of ugly plastic clogs sat by that door for going down to the garden. She slipped them on and went down the wooden steps. As she made her way around the house, she looked up at her apartment. There was nothing odd in the windows, nothing you could see from the street, and nothing in front of the door. No noise came through the windows. Still, she expected someone to come screaming out of the house after her. Who? The head, or Anne, or Ken? She needed to get away before anyone or anything could catch her, reach her, touch her. Walking as fast as she could, she kept one eye on the house for as long as possible. When she reached the corner, she checked her phone. Still nothing from Luca. Where was he? As she walked, she opened an internet browser and found his office phone number on the university's website. When he saw her number on his office phone, he would know it was serious and pick up. She scuffed along the sidewalk, checking her back and running the occasional few steps, with the phone to her ear. But it rang until Luca's voice, fifteen years younger, told her he was away from the office.

At Dabster's, she ordered an Americano with an extra shot and a slurp of cream. She took care to mock her own shoes to the kid at the cash; the kid did not care. Luca was not in the coffee shop. Should she check the washroom? While she waited for her coffee, she went to the back of the shop. But once there, she could not make herself push open the men's door. Inside the women's room, she held the door open to check the visible surfaces before venturing over the threshold. After she'd checked all the stalls, she locked herself in one, and checked her phone. Foolishly, she opened her email.

A long thread setting the date for a hiring committee meeting—staggering that people capable of advanced mathematics could not use a shared calendar—emails from undergrads she ignored, a message from Miriam, a PhD student, needing paperwork signed for her student visa, and a message from the department's executive assistant, Paula, reminding Trish about her upcoming meeting with the chair to talk strategy for research grants. Trish quelled her fury at being treated like a child by reminding herself of her colleagues' inability to plan a meeting. Tending that flock was poor Paula's bread and butter. Trish replied quickly to Miriam, telling her to leave the paper in her mailbox and that she would sign it later that day. She opened the stall and washed her hands.

Outside the cafe, standing in the sun with her coffee, Trish tried Luca's cell again and this time left a message. People looked at her as they approached the cafe and again as they left with their coffees. She smiled and shook her head, hoping to share with them the ridiculousness of her situation. One guy held the door open and raised his eyebrows at her. She shook her head, "I think I've been stood up." She finished her coffee and walked to the end of the block. Maybe Luca was coming around the corner and if she left now she would miss him. But he was not. She checked the time. It had been an hour since she'd first texted him. He didn't need an hour to get to Dabster's. Maybe he was mad at her for calling so much. He didn't know what was happening. Didn't know the urgency of the situation. She needed to find him. Campus was so close. Should she just go there now? Not to stay. Just to find Luca. But he would never come back to her apartment with her. And then she would just be alone on campus in clogs.

> You're not here. I'm going home.
> I'll come find you at work.

She checked the corner one more time and realized the head had probably been crying the whole time she was away. Maybe it had escalated to screaming by now. An hour of some unknown noise, and an especially irritating one, would definitely disturb Ken and Anne. But Trish still did not know what to do about the thing; with the thing. Even if it was still there, how was she supposed to stop it crying? On the walk home, she clutched the phone in her pocket so she would feel it vibrate when a message came in. Still, she barely put it into her pocket before she took it out to check for messages again.

CHAPTER TWO

Sure enough, when she walked back into the house, Trish could hear the thing crying. She shucked her plastic footwear gratefully and moved quickly to her bedroom. All around the head, the dresser's wood was dark with pooled tears. Poor thing was probably just as confused as Trish was. She came around to the front of the dresser and stared at the monstrosity.

Oh god, why did she have to be so alone? Why was there never anyone there for her? Why was there no one? Wait. Maybe there was no one because everyone had found one of these things? No. She'd been out in the world. There were people out there happily getting coffee. They had no disembodied heads. But Trish had gone out for coffee too. You couldn't tell by looking at someone, she assured herself. Jess. Jess had texted. Maybe Trish was abandoning poor Jess by not replying to her message. Maybe Jess needed Trish right now, too.

Trish had met and moved in with Jess in her second year of grad school. Jess was working on a PhD in political science, and she was cool. A middle-class Black woman, Jess had an ease and confidence in the world, coupled with an astute sensibility and razor-sharp wit. As a White woman in a math department, Trish was only too aware of how unworldly her redneck hometown had left her. Having Jess in her life was like an open door through which she could look out and see the world. Trish was grateful for the small shards of laughter that spilled into her. Trish still considered Jess her best friend though she knew Jess had many more important friends, and so Trish did not like to presume too much in their relationship. Besides, Jess was also new faculty—in a city several hours north of the small town where Trish had grown up. She did not need the burden of a friend who couldn't keep up.

Hey...

She couldn't think of how to announce the head's arrival. If Jess looked at her phone right now, she would see the bouncing balls. As if she would frantically be checking for messages. Still, if she happened to open her phone to Trish's message, the bubbles would be there. And Trish would look like an idiot.

HAPPY BIRTHDAY!

Hey! Thanks. How's it going there?

Is it me, or do things seem a bit off?

Haha—your world's upside down because you're thirty now.

Maybe that's it.

What's going on?

I'm not sure. Something's happened and I don't know what to make of it or what to do with it.

Do you want to talk?

No, no. I think once I get to school I'll feel better.

Okay, well let me know.

I have writing group
this morning and I
teach this afternoon
but I'm free after that.

> I'm sure it will be fine but
> a chat would be fun.

Is it that guy again?

> No. I told you that's over.
> You go write. Let's talk later.

Ok. Call if you need. I'm
in class until 4 my time.

> I'll be fine. Talk to you later.

Either Jess had no disembodied head or she was handling it just fine. Trish was on her own. She needed to figure this out. She wanted to get to the university. She wanted to find Luca, and just to feel normal. Be in a world that made sense. There was the faculty meeting anyway. What to do with this head? Calling the police or ambulance would oblige her to stay home longer—maybe even miss the meeting. And she would only have the phone to try to reach Luca, which clearly wasn't working today. She needed to leave.

But if she left this thing here, it would continue to cry. Anne upstairs was home most of the day and would hear the crying. She had lived in the building for twenty-five years and was not shy about texting Ken with problems. And Ken had a key to Trish's apartment. If the noise persisted, they might just let themselves in. Trish could not stomach the thought of them finding the head.

Maybe she could put the thing in the freezer? Anne wouldn't be able to hear it in there. And, well, wasn't it possible that the cries might stop altogether? She wobbled her head back and forth, thinking. Maybe she'd found a course of action. But then she'd have a dead head on her hands. A note of nausea at her unwitting 1970s pop culture reference. Jerry Garcia was no easier to stomach than this thing. Anyway, she did not want it dead. Imagine the courage required to take it out of the freezer, dead. Who knew how long she'd live here, but it seemed impossible she would go without ice cream the whole time. She needed to bring the thing to the university.

An image of her friend and colleague, Cam Wang, appeared in her mind's eye. Cam was the epitome of rationality. The boy spoke in statistics almost exclusively. He had very high standards of justice, which is what Trish liked about him, and he gave no truck to arguments of emotion. When a friend he secretly loved from undergrad consistently chose manipulative boyfriends, he simply refused to listen to her complain about them. He was deeply and quickly cynical about people's emotional behaviour and thought processes, as if logic and precision would rid the world of its senselessness, for everyone's betterment. There would be no talking to him about how confused and upset she felt about the head.

Trish argued with the version of Cam in her head. She had nothing to be ashamed of. It's not like she produced the head of her own volition. She had not decided on this head. Neither had she done anything to deserve it. As far as she knew. Still, it felt disgraceful, which was also ridiculous. People don't feel embarrassed by unforeseen circumstances. How could a woman be smart enough to earn a PhD in the geometry of higher dimensions but not have mastered the Newtonian basics of an emotional life?

She forced her attention back to the room. The head smacked and slurped on the dresser. Who knew vitality was so moist? Trish felt bad for the thing. If she had not done anything to deserve it, neither had the thing committed any wrongs. Imagine explaining her sympathy for the head to Cam. He would interrupt with a news story about sympathy gone awry—deceitful orphans, or internet scams. She was going to have to steel herself. This ridiculous abomination had appeared in her life. It was not her fault. No one could shame or blame her for it. Simply take it in hand, bundle it along, present it as fact. There was work to do. They couldn't stop her from doing her job simply because this mess had appeared. At the faculty meeting she would sign up for a committee. More service work could benefit her career. Especially so close to tenure. Service could be her route to tenure. Maybe she didn't need grants.

But how to carry the head?

Start with shoes—a bit of protection for handling the head. Shoes on, she strode purposefully back to her room to gather the thing, but her determination failed at the point of picking it up. Her hand hovered above its little face and a moist heat spread across her palm. Where would she put it once it was in her hand? Normally everything went into her pack. But the head might be hurt in there. Trish remembered a small black purse that her mother had given her several years ago, and she ran to dig it out of the basket of hats and scarves at the top of the closet in the front hall.

After several feints, Trish managed to graze the head with a finger. It was warm. An image flashed in her mind of her high school math teacher, Mr. Rose, his hand curled in rest on the table between them. The head's little eyes flew open as she flinched her hand away. She dug a pencil out of the bedside table, held the purse open at the edge of the dresser and used the pencil to push the head into it. As the head landed in the purse, its weight jerked her hand down and her stomach turned. The head still yelled, but at least the sound was muffled now.

Trish slung the purse crosswise over her back so that the head hung down in front. Immediately the shameful tickle of bad posture. She pulled her shoulders back sharply and secured the purse in place with her backpack. Trish never carried a purse. But every day at the university, scores of women walked around with exactly this configuration of bags on their person. Did they walk around dying of embarrassment? Was hers going to show?

She checked her phone for the time. Still nothing from Luca. But Jess had sent another message saying to call if she needed. The bus she wanted was already gone, but she could make the next one if she hurried. In a kind of bent-knee hustle, she scurried to the corner, pulling the purse down and slightly away from her body. Imagine how she looked. The bus driver was familiar and Trish smiled at him in gratitude, but he merely nodded her on. In the middle of the bus, she shuffled into a window seat, the head banging back and forth between her thighs, knocking on the hard plastic as she sat. Nothing more than it deserved. Disgusting thing. At least she had skipped the twenty minutes of torture deciding what food to bring to campus for the day, and how to get it there. Trish shook her head and looked away sharply from her reflection in the bus window. She should call her mother. Deidre would be hurt if she didn't call soon but she was not in the headspace to be happy and excited. Later—she would have to call later.

As soon as the bus turned into campus, the head started to cry and was shrieking inside its purse by the time Trish opened the door to the faculty meeting. All thirty-five or so people at the table turned.

From the head of the table, the department chair, Wei Tang, said, "Oh Trish! There…"

But she didn't get any further. The noise was overwhelming.

"Trish, what's going on?"

Trish gave a little smile, as though she'd just walked in and farted. Somehow, even though the head cried almost constantly, Trish had not imagined how the crying would affect the faculty meeting. She'd only imagined that she would show the head to Luca and maybe Cam at a time of her choosing, and that she would be the one crying, or calm. Of course, though, the head had taken these options from her.

Well, didn't she have a right to a personal life? What did this thing hanging from her body have to do with her ability to contribute to a faculty meeting? She stared at the floor as she made her way to an open seat between two Russian colleagues, who pushed their chairs away from the noise coming from her purse.

"Trish?" Tang tried again.

It was too much. Why was Tang on her like this? Trish was crying. She struggled out of her pack and coat—it was just so hot—before she leaned her elbows on the table and buried her face in her hands.

"Oh god, I don't know, I don't know, I don't know."

Between the two of them, the head and Trish filled the room with noise, and the table of mostly men exchanged looks of confusion and frustration. The department's executive assistant, Paula, left the room and returned with tissues and water, which she placed on the table in front of Trish.

"Thank you," Trish looked up and whispered.

Manners—truly rooted in our simian need for acceptance.

"Trish, what's happening?"

"I don't …"

She couldn't say it, couldn't make herself say the words that needed to be said. Showing them was the only option. If they saw the thing, they would know that she wasn't disturbing the meeting on purpose. That she had done nothing wrong. They would see that this thing was beyond her and that she needed help. The head would not be quiet. With the sleeve of her sweatshirt pulled down over her hand, Trish reached into the purse in front of her. Squeezing her eyes shut, she made herself feel for the back of the head. As she cupped the little thing, it stopped crying. Once it was out of the purse, Trish opened her eyes and placed the head gently on the table in front of her. It immediately began to cry again. A kind of repetitive whiney, stumbling, tripping sound. The Russians on either side of her pushed themselves away from the table. In fact, most of them pushed away from the table. A couple leaned in closer. One or two people left the room.

"What is that?" Tang exploded from the front.

"I don't know!" Trish wailed, throwing herself back in her chair. "It was there on my dresser when I got out of the shower this morning."

"*This* was on your dresser?" repeated Tang.

"YES!"

These were skilled, capable, intelligent people. Surely, they could help.

The head had gone quiet, but its little face continued to work. The face was not quite right. Needless to say. It bulged. It was pudgy and slack but was in constant motion.

"I heard it while I was in the shower and when I went into my room it was there. Crying."

"Why did you bring it here?" asked Tang.

"What else was I supposed to do with it? I couldn't just leave it there. The neighbours."

Tang raised her eyebrows.

"It was crying!"

"Okay… Well… Look…" Tang tried again, but really, she'd come to her leadership position for her publication record, not the presence of any actual leadership skills. "You can't very well be here with it. Why don't you take it home? Take it and go home for the day." She flapped her hand toward the door.

"WHAT?" Trish practically screamed and so did not hear what Tang said next.

"Don't bring it back," Tang's flapping hand firmed into a stop sign.

"No. You can't make me go home with it. I can't be alone with it. I'll lose my bloody mind. No. NO. I need to stay here. I need to be with you. You need to help me. You need to help me with this."

"Trish," said Luca across the table. He stood, "Come on. Let's get a coffee."

"Yes," agreed Tang. "Thanks, Luca."

Trish was also relieved. Why had she not thought of that? She should have just beckoned Luca from the door. She scooped the head up on the cuffs of her sleeves and dropped it back into the purse before grabbing her pack and coat. Across the table, Cam gave her a look of concern and she gave him a small, sad, smile before following Luca out of the conference room. The weight of the fleshy thing banged against her stomach as she walked.

As the door closed behind her, Trish pleaded with Luca, "God, I'm so sorry."

"What the hell is going on with you today?"

Luca glanced back into the conference room and then

directed her further down the hall, away from the glass wall. He always knew to do things like that.

"I called you!"

"Yeah, four times!"

"You didn't answer."

"Because I couldn't talk! I was in the middle of something with Sheila. You calling like a maniac did not help."

"I'm sorry. I didn't know, obviously. I know you need space. I'm sorry. I don't want to upset you."

"Okay. Hey, don't worry." He blew air through his pursed lips. "It can't get any worse with Sheila."

"She's crazy to leave you. It sucks."

"What the hell's happening, anyway?" He rubbed his hand hard across his forehead. He looked tired. Inside the purse, the head shrieked.

"This thing!" Trish gestured to the wailing purse. "It just showed up this morning and I don't know what it is, or where it came from, and I don't know what to do. All I could think was to come here. I thought I could work. What else am I supposed to do? But it's so distracting. I can't think. What am I supposed to do?" Trish was crying again.

"It's quite the racket."

"I know you want space. I just don't know who else... I have no one else, Luca!"

The truth of the statement struck Trish, wretched thing. So pathetic that she had to disrespect the wishes of one of her very few friends precisely because he was one of her very few friends. Alienate him as a function of her own utter alienation.

"No, no. C'mon. You know I'm here for you. Look, let's get the hell out of this place." He looked behind him toward the elevators, back past the conference room's glass wall. "Here," he pointed with his chin over her head. "Let's take the stairs."

CHAPTER THREE

In the Student Union Building, Luca pointed to a table and went to buy coffee. Trish pulled the purse off her shoulder and put it on the table. Freedom from the weight of the head brought enormous relief and the familiarity of SUB for coffee with Luca was lovely.

Trish met Luca on her first day at Cascadia. His office was directly across the hall from hers. Paula had walked Trish to her office and handed her the key. Luca's door stood open, and he came out to introduce himself.

"Let me know if you need anything."

The math department was in a brand-new interdisciplinary science building with floor-to-ceiling windows in the offices along the exterior walls. But those offices had all been occupied already and Trish was assigned an office in the middle of the building, without any windows to the outside. The wall that faced the hallway was frosted glass and the sunlight through Luca's office let in a blue glow. An L-shaped desk sat in the middle of the room. Trish unpacked a box of books and opened and closed the drawers on the filing cabinet and the desk. Finally, she sat in the chair behind the desk. All she could see was the wall in front of her. She pushed herself around in the wheeled chair. If the desk was against the glass wall, she could catch a glimpse of an outside window down the hall.

She braced a hip against the edge of the desk and pushed. One leg of the L juddered away from its companion, and she pulled on the laggard leg and stood to assess her work. An inch of progress.

"Hey," she tapped on Luca's still-open door.

"Hey!" He pushed away from a page of text on his screen and swivelled in his chair to face her. "How's it going?"

"I could stand some help. If you have a second?"

"Sure," he rubbed his hands together. "What do you need?"

Behind the larger of the two sides of the desk, he tucked his tie in between two buttons near the top of his shirt. His collar stood out from his neck.

"You take that side, so we don't pull them apart."

Then he put a hand on either side of the desk and picked the whole thing up. Trish tottered behind with the other side of the desk. Luca put the desk down where Trish indicated, pulled the chair over and sat.

"Oh yeah, this'll be great. Very nice. Have a seat." He held the chair out for her. "Hey, you want a coffee? I have one of those pod machines in my office."

He brought in two mugs of coffee and set one in front of Trish. It read, *I'm not perfect, but I'm Italian.*

She looked up at him sharply, "Why did you give me this one?"

Luca held up the other mug, "This one's from a computational math conference. I gave you the more interesting one."

"I'd do computational math if I could."

"Small mercies. Those guys are deadly boring."

If Luca was Italian, he knew Trish was Italian. He did not need to know that her father was the least interesting person she'd ever known.

Three of Luca's fingers covered the mug. The skin on his hands was rough.

"Where does a mathematician get hands like that?"

"Ah, these ugly things," he squeezed a hand open and closed and then ignored the question.

"So, are you just coming from a postdoc, or …?"

His hair was grey at the temples and thinning on top, but he hadn't taken the route of shaving it bald. It stood up in soft spikes.

Later that week, Trish offered him cookies from her lunch and the next Friday, when he was gone early, he emailed her to say goodbye. One morning, about a month after Trish started, his door stood open when she came back from teaching.

"Hey Luca," she called as she opened her door.

He appeared in his doorway, "Hey, come here for a sec."

Trish expected he wanted her to laugh at the stupidity of an email he'd received. She took the key out of her door and followed him into his office. He closed the door most of the way behind him and gestured Trish to the chair by his desk where his grad students sat to complain. He rolled his own chair over in front of her and leaned forward, elbows on knees.

"Listen, I like you."

Her face grew hot. "I like you, too."

"I'm married."

"I know."

"But I was thinking …"

Her heart clenched. His bravery was impressive. She would not equivocate either.

"I was thinking that we could have some fun together. Nothing serious. But it could be fun to, you know, get together."

"Yeah, okay."

"Think about it."

"I just did. I want to. Have some fun."

"Alright," Luca rocked back in his chair, smiling widely.

Trish stood and went back to her office.

Later, as the sun set, Luca's face appeared in her doorway, "C'mere."

His office door clicked shut behind her and he pressed her against the suit jackets hanging on the back of his door.

They settled into a routine of fooling around in Luca's office after hours, with afternoons at the campus hotel maybe once a month. Trish paid for the hotel because Luca's wife had access to his credit card records. He dropped cash on her desk to cover his share.

Never had she known a lover who wanted to take so much time with the act. It irritated her. She always wanted to orgasm quickly so that the man might feel free to do the same, and they could be done. Once she orgasmed, she did not want to feel anything further, and could not stand touch beyond the necessary penetration. But Luca wanted to take his time. If something felt good, he wanted it to go on. And he wanted her to continue to pay attention to him, even after she orgasmed. Given that they were paying for the hotel room, it made sense to take their time, but Trish was very much used to wanting to get it over with. It took her several getaways to learn not to orgasm too quickly. The extended periods of stimulation were annoying, but Luca stayed affectionate even after they made love, which soothed the irritation. They would work through math problems and talk office politics. It was nice to think about math with Luca's heavy arm draped across her belly.

"Why are your hands so big?" she asked as they lay facing each other, intertwining their fingers through different patterns.

That first time, he only told her that he boxed, and that he paid his way through university, from BSc to PhD with boxing matches. Later he told her that he boxed to capitalize on the fighting skill he'd needed as a kid in Verona. His father owned an Iso Autocarro—a half ton pickup truck with an egg-shaped cab and bubble windows—for delivering dry goods. He would drop Luca off at the men's prison with the truck, leaving him responsible for finding someone to drive while Luca sold the wares and defended the truck from other kids who tried to steal from it along the route. More than one of the men raped him in the back of the truck.

"I still can't go into fabric stores."

He brushed away her sympathy.

"My father grew up in Verona," Trish finally admitted.

"I thought I might be telling you things you already know."

Even from the little her father had said, Trish knew Verona was rough. But Luca had learned to fight defending the dry goods truck from kids of all sizes and even some adults. And he had used the habit to get ahead, build a life for himself. Trish's father, on the other hand, had responded to the poundings of his youth with petulance and the mere feeling of being put upon for the rest of his life.

Now Luca came back to their table at SUB, and Trish accepted the steaming paper cup from him and took a sip. Inside the purse on the table, the head began to cry. People were glancing and staring. One woman flinched as she passed. Trish smiled an apology.

"This is so awkward," she hissed to Luca. "The noise. God."

Luca's brow was tight. "Where did you find this thing?"

"It was just there on my dresser this morning after I got out of the shower."

Luca shook his head, confused. "Was anything taken? Did you call the cops?"

Trish leaned in closer and lowered her voice.

"I think it showed up on its own." Even as she spoke, the absurdity of the statement stung. "I know that's ridiculous."

Luca raised his eyebrows, his lips curled. "It's the least likely scenario. So, you did not call the police. Don't you think you might have called the police instead of ringing me like a madwoman."

"I'm sorry, Luca. Really. You're the only one I could think to call." Even if he knew how profoundly alone she was, he would not have been more sympathetic. "The police are not going to take this thing seriously."

"Well, you're not exactly helping yourself."

Trish's head hung with the knowledge of her shame. "The only thing I can think is that someone hates me."

"Yeah," Luca tilted his cup in consideration.

"Andrew hates me." The truth reminded Trish that she'd never replied to this morning's email chain.

"No." Luca shook his head and sipped his coffee. "I mean, yes, he hates you. But he wouldn't send you something this horrible."

"What makes you so sure? I nearly ordered him a bag of dicks."

Andrew Wagner was the department's current associate chair responsible for undergraduate programs, a position for which he felt himself profoundly overqualified. Trish sat on the undergraduate curriculum committee, which consisted of herself and a very old white man. Andrew was the chair of the committee and vouched no input other than his own. Andrew would not even ask the old white guy to do any work, instead turning to Trish and saying, "Trish, you don't mind typing that up for us." Once he asked Trish to write an email to faculty members soliciting their input on prerequisites for the honours program and send it to him for approval first, which she "accidentally" sent straight to the faculty email list. He came tap-tapping down the hall in his shiny brown dress shoes, pastel tie but no jacket, and closed the door to her office saying that he would have given the request to one of the "girls" interning in the office but had presumed it would be safe with Trish because she "had a PhD or whatever." How, in the face of administrative resistance, a math degree from Caltech turns into a "PhD or whatever," Trish didn't understand, and said so. Andrew in turn noted that math was a small community and that there were only so many people who could evaluate her grant proposals, even at the national level. Trish assured him that her publication record spoke for itself, which it did at the time. He replied that she certainly wasn't earning any service points for her tenure application, and stormed out, slamming the door behind him. Trish took advantage of the privacy to find a vendor of penis-shaped gummy candies and was ordering the biggest bag to send to Andrew's departmental mailbox when Luca knocked on her door and interrupted the scheme with good sense.

"He shouldn't have threatened you, but it's true—the math world is small."

For six months, Andrew managed to run the undergraduate curriculum review committee without speaking to her.

Across from her in SUB, Luca shook his head. "He's too wily to endanger himself like that."

A wave of realization poured over Trish. "Luca! Sheila! Sheila hates me!"

Luca sat back forcefully in his chair and held his palms out in front of him. "No. No. You leave Sheila out of this. Do not bring Sheila into your crazy thing here, whatever it is. No."

She felt the need to have Luca at least cede her logic. "It's a possibility. Boiled rabbits and such."

"No. No. Sadly, you're not in a movie, for one thing. Sheila doesn't even know you exist, for another. And she could never," he gestured to the bag on the table. "She could never handle such a thing."

"She didn't have to. She had it delivered."

Luca took a deep breath and put his fists on his hips.

"You need to stop. You do not know Sheila. She would never conceive of such a thing. Leave her out of this."

"She doesn't even know I exist?"

Luca threw his hands in the air and looked around the room. "I don't want to get divorced!"

Inside the purse on the table, the head began to cry again. Sweat sprang into Trish's pits. Her bra stuck to her skin. She moaned and slid the bag off the table into her lap and curled over it.

"Were you drunk?"

"No. I was just at home. The night before I turned thirty and I was asleep before eleven!"

"Oh god, it's your birthday, isn't it? Sorry. Jeez. Happy birthday."

Trish waved away his apology and good wishes. Her birthday no longer seemed at all relevant. "What if no one sent it? What do you think it means? I really need some help."

"Means? Nothing. It's probably what you said—someone hates you. Okay, look. I just thought of something. In the alley outside my gym downtown, there are no cameras. Tonight after dark, take it down there, and toss it into one of the big blue garbage cans. I can meet you there. About eight-thirty. Just chuck it."

The idea of meeting Luca after dark in an alley behind his boxing gym was deeply appealing. Trish liked the idea of having access to that part of his life. "I can't. I'm really scared."

"It doesn't have to be such a big deal. Look, this thing's freaky. But you're the one making such a big deal. If it were me, I'd just say fuck it and forget it. Just forget it."

"Luca, it's really upsetting, it's scary. Even if I dumped it at your gym, or behind your gym or whatever, I'd still be scared but then I'd be looking over my shoulder all the time."

"Look, you need to be rational. There's nothing to be afraid of—it can't hurt you. If you threw it away, you would begin to forget about it."

Trish shook her head. "Look, it's alive. There's some modicum of obligation. There's something about the fact of its existence. I can't just determine the thing is offensive because it offends our sense of what we think is *right*," Trish drew air quotes and rolled her eyes.

"Eternal truths are elegant. This thing is not."

"There are unknowable truths." She made one final defense of her position. But she knew she could not argue with Luca based on the feeling in her gut, her sense of this thing. "I know how it looks. I just want someone with me. It's so disgusting. I feel embarrassed by it. Like I did this somehow. I can't believe I have to haul this thing around now. If someone was with me, then I wouldn't feel so ashamed!"

Luca raised an eyebrow and sipped his coffee. "You have your meeting with Tang tomorrow, eh?"

Untenured faculty met yearly with the department chair to discuss their progress toward tenure. The meetings had not been a big deal the first couple of years Trish was at Cascadia.

She had publications, and the university had given her some awards to set up her research group. Even last year, she was still waiting to hear about her grant, so there was promise. Potential. But none of her grants had come through. That alone set back her progress and then the knock-on effects piled up. Because she didn't have funding, she couldn't attract grad students, and because she didn't have grad students, she wasn't producing papers, and because she wasn't producing papers, her grant applications weren't any stronger, and so her tenure application also grew weaker because it ought to have been growing stronger. Lately all her energy had been taken up thinking of new lines of research that might secure funding. Tang had been excited to tell Trish about a fashion designer who used geometry for a season. Trish was trying to think of ways to apply geometry of higher dimensions to the climate crisis. So far, she'd only come up with some examples to give to her students. Tang had promised to talk strategy in Trish's meeting tomorrow.

"I was fine until this thing showed up." On her lap, the head was quiet, but she could feel minute movements, which infuriated her. Why could the thing not keep still? She took a long pull of coffee and let the heat sear a passage through her throat and chest.

"Listen darling, it's awful that this has happened to you. But it's not serving you to be here. It's not like you're going to be able to work. You need to go home and take care of yourself."

"Oh god, no. I can't be alone with this thing. I have to work. I have a paper I'm working on, and Brandon gave me something to read. Miriam needs some immigration form signed." Trish looked behind her to the door out of SUB that led to the math building. "I need to do that. It's the crying. And it's just so repulsive."

She pushed her shoulder blades into the chair back—a vain attempt to put space between herself and the head—gravity kept the thing pressed to her lap. There was no backing away. Her sweat had grown cold. Now she was just damp and shivering.

"This thing can't matter. It's not like they can keep me from my job just because I have this thing. Women have babies and they get to keep their jobs. They even bring them to campus!" She opened her arms and hands wide to show that what she said was demonstrably true and to show her admiration for the practice. Less the practice, really, than the capability.

Luca's eyes widened and he looked around. "Where do you see children?"

"You see them! They come to campus. Tang's kids were in the department a couple weekends ago!"

"You see them occasionally and people put up with it occasionally. But this is a place of work. No one expects to have to deal with whatever the hell you've got going on in your personal life." Luca flapped a disgusted hand at Trish's whimpering lap.

"I didn't choose this. It's not my fault."

Luca softened. "Come on. I know. You don't have to tell me that. You would never choose this. But now it's your responsibility."

"If it's not my fault, then how come I have to deal with it on my own?"

Luca shrugged, "Habeas caput."

Trish was done. She gathered everything under one arm, the head screaming inside the purse. Standing, she took one last sip of coffee and put the cup down in front of Luca. "Thanks for nothing."

"Trish, come on."

But she didn't stop, and Luca didn't move.

The mailroom was empty, fortunately. But Trish's mailbox was stuffed with papers. On top was Miriam's immigration form. Underneath that was a CV for someone she didn't know. A stack of resumes. Oh god. The hiring committee. They were hiring for a position in representation theory, a field that transformed abstract structures into linear spaces. Higher dimensions and manifolds are fundamental to the field, which was why Trish was on the committee.

"I know you need time for research right now," Tang had sympathized. "But you're the only high dimension geometry person we have, so we kind of need you."

Trish flipped through the stapled papers.

"Oh good. I was going to email you to make sure you picked those up."

Abasa Abara, who chaired the hiring committee, stood beside her. The man was utterly useless, which was probably why they'd given him this assignment. Typically, he wandered the halls all day looking for open office doors so he might go in and hold forth, in a remarkably shrill voice, about various injustices wrought upon his career by the university's central administration.

Trish had alienated the man early in her time at Cascadia, telling him that she could not see his point about recent changes to the department's website. She was entirely uninterested in the question of the website. But his position was that the department's decision to use it to attract students, instead of using it as a kind of internal newsletter, struck her as apparently illogical, and she told him so. After that he would not even look at her if they passed in the halls. Everyone begrudged Abasa coming into their offices, so Trish wore his scorn as a badge of honour.

Abasa had been displeased about having Trish on the hiring committee for this new position. She presumed he hoped the candidate would replace her, and her presence on the committee only spoke to her importance.

"You didn't reply to my email about the meeting," Abara accused.

He glanced quickly down at the purse hanging in front of Trish. A shot of heat pierced her belly and spread to her face. Abasa rested his crossed arms on the ledge of his belly.

Behind him the door opened, and voices poured in from the hallway. The faculty meeting had come to an end. Four, five, six of Trish's colleagues pushed into the mailroom, still deep in discussion, shouting and laughing. As they noticed her there, with Abara, they fell silent. Most, in fact, just continued straight through and left again by the other door. Trish waited until Yu Xang had retrieved his mail and made a show of leaving on tiptoes.

"I didn't want to clutter everyone's inboxes."

Maybe that would teach him to use a shared calendar. Trish took one last look in her mailbox and turned to leave.

"How am I supposed to know you will do your work, if you don't answer emails?"

Trish squinted at him and then walked away without answering. She was pretty sure she didn't have to answer to Abara.

As she turned the corner, she saw her grad student, Brandon, leaning against the glass wall of her office.

"Oh shit, sorry. Have you been waiting long?" Yesterday afternoon Trish had agreed to meet Brandon after the faculty meeting.

"No, no."

She felt lighter seeing someone with whom she was working toward some common goal. Brandon was one of Trish's few successes. Mostly she'd had master's students, which were good, but of a lower grade than PhD students. Brandon had chosen Cascadia for his PhD in order to work with Trish. He was a stellar student, and it gave Trish some cachet.

"Do you still have time? I just want to talk about the manifold problem I told you about."

"Yeah, God, thinking about math would be nice. Just gimme a sec."

Struggling with the CVs and the purse and her pack, Trish finally got the office door open. She dropped the CVs on her desk and threw her pack on the floor. Brandon lowered himself into the chair beside her desk and watched her efforts with raised eyebrows. Finally, Trish flopped into her chair and threw herself against the back.

"PHEW!" She let out a giant sigh of relief.

"You okay?"

Suddenly, Trish thought Brandon might know about the head. He might understand and know where it came from. Maybe it was a thing that younger people knew about. Maybe Trish was just at that cusp and had been touched by it but didn't understand. She leaned forward in her chair. "Can I ask you about something?"

"Suuure …"

She closed her office door most of the way, letting the catch rest against the frame. "This thing has happened."

"Okay."

"And I don't understand it."

Brandon's eyes were wide.

"I've asked Luca, Professor Marino," she gestured out the window to Luca's office across the hall. "But he doesn't know."

"If Professor Marino doesn't know…" Brandon shook his head to indicate that he probably could not help Trish.

Maybe she shouldn't show it to Brandon. If he presumed Luca knew more than he did, he probably presumed she knew more than he did, too. Asking him a question changed that and made her less intelligent than Luca. And Brandon! He might presume she was less intelligent. He might presume that already. Probably because she was a woman. But wasn't it a sign of intelligence to know when you don't know something? And a sign of character to be able to ask? Yes, she could show Brandon that asking for help was not a sign of weakness. Besides, no one had helped yet and he might know the answer. And how was she supposed to find out whether or not he knew the answer if she didn't even ask. He didn't have to know. He didn't have to say anything. He could just ask her to put it back in her purse and they could go on talking about math.

"No, but maybe it's something young people are doing. I'll show you. It's a bit weird. A bit freaky."

"I'm really confused."

"It's maybe a bit upsetting. If it is, that's cool. That's okay. You just tell me, and we don't have to talk about it."

Brandon nodded, his brow deeply furrowed.

She took the purse strap from over her head and held the purse open so Brandon could look inside. He sat forward in his seat and peered in. His face knotted and he sat back in his chair silently.

"What do you think?"

"Uh. I don't know what to think."

"It was there on my dresser when I woke up. Well not exactly. I was in the shower." Was that true? Had it been there when she woke up? Just because she hadn't noticed it, doesn't mean it wasn't there. "Well. I think I was in the shower. I don't know. Have you ever seen anything like it?"

Brandon was silent, his eyes wide. He shook his head slowly.

"No. Fuck—me neither! What kind of monstrosity is this, hey?"

But Brandon would not talk.

"I guess you didn't need to see that. I just don't know what it is and, like, where did it come from? Does someone hate me?" Trish's hands shook.

"Yeah," Brandon was standing, his pack hoisted onto one shoulder. "That's a lot."

"Oh god, sorry. You wanted to talk about your 3-manifolds. Let's do that." Trish put the purse with the head on top of her filing cabinet and sat, gesturing to the chair Brandon had been in.

"No, no. That's okay. You have a lot going on."

"Are you sure? Cuz I don't really. You'd be saving me from looking at all those CVs."

Brandon gave a weak smile.

"Do you want to meet early tomorrow before class to talk?"

When Brandon first started to TA for Trish, he had come to her office before class a few times to talk about the course and his work, and then they had walked over to the lecture hall together. After they no longer needed the meetings, Brandon still met Trish at her office, and they walked over together. Miriam was also a TA, but she was always already in a seat at the front of the lecture hall when they arrived.

Miriam. Her form. "Oh. Hey. Remind me to bring Miriam's immigration form tomorrow."

Brandon's eyes looked off to the right as he nodded.

"Come early. We'll talk about the manifolds!"

From the doorway Brandon looked back, "Sure."

And he was gone, walking very quickly, his head bent.

On the bus ride home, Trish's phone rang in her pack. Her mother. Her birthday. Trish had forgotten entirely to call her mother.

"I expected to hear from you," Deidre said when Trish answered.

"Yeah, sorry. Work's a bit busy these days."

"At least you get to see people when you're busy. I've been holed up in the studio painting for days. I was looking forward to your call to break things up for me."

After she'd heard what her mother was working on and for whom, Trish ended the call with the birthday goodbye, "Thanks for giving birth to me."

And her mother's reply, "Let's just be grateful that day is over."

Trish threw the phone deep into her pack and realized she was unbearably hungry. She should cook something. Make use of her time. If she planned better, she could cook more often.

An image of Miriam's government form sitting on top of the stack of CVs appeared in her mind's eye. Damnit. Should she turn around? Get off the bus and walk back? She could eat at SUB. Too complicated. Sign the form tomorrow.

Noodles. She would eat noodles. Swallow huge scoopfuls of them. Barely chew the salty, yellow, and green-flecked, glutinous mass before forcing it down her throat, the mass scouring her esophagus as it went down and the word *bolus* bounced around her brain.

On the living room couch, the sun slanting through the window, Trish ate the noodles staring into the middle distance. The head bawled in its purse on the kitchen table. In a moment of mercy, after she'd eaten, the thing fell silent, and Trish fell asleep on the couch.

An enormous noise roared through the air, and she was on her feet and running, calling out, "Mum! Mum! Mum!" before she was even fully awake. She stopped and stood. It was the head crying from its purse in the kitchen. Why had she called for her mother like that? Some aspect of her child self had acquired a new degree of freedom, clearly. Cocooned in the heavy ooze of sleep, she was ravenous again. Holding the wall for support, she tottered to the kitchen, flipping open the purse flap so that the thing could get air. It continued to cry.

At the kitchen table she sat with a bucket of yoghurt and a spoon. As she came to, she pulled the purse onto her lap and the cries slowed. Trish slid her laptop closer to her across the table and searched the internet for "small heads, sudden appearance," but all she got were makeup tips and porn. She closed the computer and finished the yoghurt and just sat in the quiet, the clock above the sink ticking, as the sky outside the window faded from violet to black.

The thing needed a place to sleep for the night. Trish could not keep it against her like this. Her eyes fell on the tea towel draped through the fridge's handle. Yes.

She kept her gum in the dish towel drawer and the smell of mint wafted up as she rifled through the drawer, feeling for the softest cloth. Most of her dishcloths were a waffled red and green cotton—a bit rough for the little thing. A couple that were white with black polka dots, were softer, but they were pretty thin and maybe not that cozy. Finally, she found an old dishcloth of her mother's that she had somehow ended up with. It was not waffled but was still thicker than Trish's white ones, even though it was older. Even the responsibility of dishcloths was too much for her.

After she finished digging around, the cloths were vaguely nest-shaped, which struck Trish as ideal. Make a nest for the head. Maybe the linen closet was a better idea? Cozier? But no, what if Ken and Anne's linen closets were lined up with hers? The sound of the head's cries would travel through the air shaft. Well, the drawer would work. They used to keep babies in drawers. The building's kitchens were stacked for the plumbing, so the thing would be tucked away in a corner of the building, far from anyone's bedroom. If it started to cry, Trish could just turn on the dishwasher. She folded a couple of the waffled towels on the bottom of the drawer, covered with her mother's soft cloth and banked the nest with the remaining cloths. Trish stood back and rubbed her hands together. The soft shadows and peaks struck her as brilliant.

She took her hysterical purse from the kitchen table and placed it in the drawer with the opening at the edge of her newly hatched nest. Then she poured and slid the head out of the purse onto the nest. The banks worked and caught the head's initial roll, sending it briefly up and then slowing its fall so it landed without too much agitation. Still the thing cried. Trish jiggled the bottom cloth a bit to make sure its mouth and nose weren't buried. Then she stood, hands on hips, watching it cry. The towels would not only muffle the sound but also absorb moisture. Happy realization. There was nothing more she could do. And she needed to get away from it.

The thing stopped crying when she closed the drawer, and Trish stared down at the handle, holding her breath and hoping. But it started again, and Trish's shoulders drooped. She stood listening, assessing the noise. The drawer underneath the head's nest was large and largely empty. It was meant for baking equipment, bowls or even a mixer, of which Trish had none. The drawer housed a few rarely used cookie cutters, two plastic water bottles, one of their caps, and a plastic travel mug. A drawer of environmental shame. She imagined the head's cries as waves crashing against the big drawer's sides, shaking the plastic before they travelled across Ken's ceiling. Anne would hear less.

When she opened it, the big bottom drawer released cries into the kitchen. The water bottles could be recycled. The cap could stay. From the linen closet she retrieved several bath towels and a top sheet she never used, carried everything into the kitchen and stuffed it all into the drawer, covering the lone green plastic cap. When she closed the drawer, the head's cries were more muffled. Still, in order to face Calculus 100 at ten o'clock, she needed sleep. She locked the dishwasher door and pushed the button for a regular cycle. First the plastic and now the dishwasher.

On the bedside table, Trish's phone lit up with Jess's name and her heart sank. Should she answer it? It was her birthday after all. Any reasonable person would be out with friends. Jess would think so, too. As a reasonable person. But Trish had asked for help, and Jess had been kind enough to keep her word. Maybe talking to Jess would help. Wasn't that what people said? Talking to people helped. Clearing her throat, Trish quickly asked Jess how teaching had gone.

"So, what's going on? What are you scared about?"

"Scared? Nothing. I'm not scared. I'm sitting at home on my thirtieth birthday. Not amazing but not scary."

"You said you were scared."

"No. It's okay. I just … you know, it's a big birthday. I freaked out."

"Listen, I've been in my thirties for like three years now, and it's the best. I promise. You'll love it."

"I'm honestly not that worried."

"How's that paper you were working on? Curves beyond time?"

"Not beyond time. The higher dimensions are all about

collapse and evolution… modelling that from different per-
spectives…" Trish trailed off. She needed urgently to talk
about the head. "I'm wondering if I'm seeing things? Like
making things up?"

"Your stuff always sounds made up to me. I love it."

"Well, but if the world is deeply hostile…?"

"Not with your publication record, it's not."

"My publication record is like a piece of paper floating on
a vast sea of hostility."

"See. Trish. There is no sea of hostility. That's just how hard
you push yourself. You tell yourself you're at the bottom of
the ocean but just because you say so, doesn't make it true."

"You're right. I know. I'm fine." In bed, she began to cry.
Thick tears stuck to her cheeks, and the word *gelatinous* again,
and then *vicious*, and finally *fiasco*, swam through her mind.

CHAPTER FOUR

The next morning, Trish woke up with the familiar, dread-tinged disappointment that she was no longer asleep. Hard not to dread early morning classes. While the coffee perked, she sat at the kitchen table and stared at the head's drawer. Maybe the thing had disappeared overnight? It had appeared suddenly. Maybe it would also disappear suddenly. Maybe some spatial axis had folded, rendering the thing out of perspective. She was not going to open the drawer yet, in any case. After yesterday, she deserved a coffee on the balcony.

As the coffee cleared her head, she began to consider what she would do with the head at work. If she left it in the office, it would just cry. A colleague once left his six-year-old son locked in his office while he worked with students in the computer lab. When the kid started to cry, the whole department heard it. While several of the department's senior members marvelled at what an impossible situation the man had been put in, to care reasonably for his son AND fulfill his work obligations, Paula was tasked with minding the child in her own office, which had done little for her sympathies toward the professor. Given the power of the administrator in an academic's life, leaving the thing alone in Trish's office was not an option.

Well, Brandon had seen it yesterday and that hadn't been a big deal. She would bring it with her and just keep it in the purse—put it on the little shelf inside the lectern. And if students made a big deal about the noise, that was their problem, wasn't it? Maybe they would finally understand that a constant hum of chatter is distracting when a person's trying to work. If they found the noise distracting, they could concentrate harder. Same with the meeting with Tang. Trish could concentrate with this thing hanging around her neck. If Tang couldn't, then that was on her. Regardless of what was happening in her personal life, Trish had the right to be taken seriously at work.

When she came in from the porch, she put her mug quietly in the sink, listening hard for noises from the drawer. She heard small movements, like a hamster burrowing under shavings and shredded tissue. Quiet enough.

At the end of the tub, Trish redirected the cool water away from her body. The phrase *scene of the crime* echoed through her mind. As she shampooed her hair, a sensation like a bubble or a pocket of air began to expand in her belly. The pressure pushed itself up into her head and suddenly she remembered a recurring nightmare from childhood. The fear exploded into her as though she was six again and just awake from the dream; in it, she woke up and, at the other end of her room, beside her dresser, stood a little man, but not a human. Trish thought of him as a troll. The troll stood beside her dresser and with his right hand bounced a red rubber ball. The ball was not nice. The red paint was dull and chipped, the black foam rubber was cheap and hard. She imagined her parents had played with such toys in the sixties. The troll smiled while he bounced the ball. The corners of his mouth were tight, and one side pulled up while the other pulled down, and he would exhale sharply through his nose, shaking his head the tiniest bit. It was as if he knew something she didn't, or as though he knew she was scared and found that funny and gratifying.

She had to lie down and go back to sleep while he was still in the room, bouncing his ball. The image of the troll by her dresser haunted her while she was awake, too. In school, the image would rise, unbidden before her mind's eye. The revulsion for that rubber ball burned through her arms and legs while a sense of certitude settled in her belly that reality was not friendly.

As she rinsed the shampoo from her eyes, she could not believe she had forgotten the dream. It, and the certainty of reality's underbelly, informed her understanding of the world for many years. The world was filled with malicious intent from the near and far sides of the unknown. When had she forgotten? Why had she forgotten? What had so mollified her? Had her ability to manipulate higher dimensions, their shadows and projections, placated her? Made her think she was in control? Now there was the evidence of the head. Trish had been fooled. Had fooled herself. The world was deeply unknown and frightening. Had she not just said so to Jess last night? A sea of hostility. Trish, a floating sheaf of paper. As a child, she knew that the main significance of the strangeness of the world was the depth of her aloneness. Alone to face the contemptuous strangeness. Trish reminded herself that she had her meeting with Tang. She was grateful to be going somewhere where she knew what was expected of her.

She put off dealing with the head until right before she was ready to leave. With her shoes and coat on, and the purse already across her shoulder, she went into the kitchen to retrieve the thing.

When she opened the drawer, she could not figure out what she was looking at. The head was there, moving and giving off slight sounds. But it had turned onto its side; half the face was turned away and the half that was up was covered slightly with cloth. Trish used a fingernail to move the cloth off the top of the head. But doing so only caused the head to roll further forward.

"Hey, what's going on?" she asked.

It wouldn't be able to breathe like that. Trish tugged on the cloth with her thumb and index finger. It was oddly resistant, heavy. The cloth was probably tucked around the head. But as she pulled, the head hung from the towel. It was stuck. Trish held the towel up so the head was eye level above the open drawer.

"Oh god. What is happening?"

The head had the towel in its mouth and was sucking on it hard enough to support its own weight. If the head weighed a pound, which was Trish's best guess from carrying the damned thing around yesterday, then it was exerting a force of a half Newton to support itself like that. A ring of damp spread into the towel around the little mouth.

Trish grabbed another towel from the drawer to support it from underneath and moved the suckling head to the countertop. She crouched down and watched. A mild sense of pride rose through her. The thing had found its own solution. It put her in mind of Mr. Rose's slow smile when she showed him her work.

As she watched, it dawned on her. Suckling. The head might be hungry. It hadn't occurred to her that it might need to eat. But where would the food go? Still, if the thing experienced hunger, Trish did not want to contribute to its suffering. She took one of the towels from the drawer and held it to the open milk spout as she tipped it. The milk seeped into the towel as Trish watched the head as though it might dash out the door before she could offer it the milk. How to get the towel out of its mouth? Trish tugged. Nothing. So, she took another towel and held the head steady as she yanked more firmly and popped the towel out of the head's mouth. The head smacked its little lips. Cute. Then Trish offered it the twist of milk-soaked towel, which it took in eagerly and suckled twice before spilling it back onto the counter, its little nose scrunched right up to its forehead. Once could be happenstance. Any scientist knows that. Trish twisted the towel into a nib again and held it to the head's mouth and again it took the towel in and sucked a couple of times before the head's pink oyster tongue oozed it back out to the counter. A drop of white stayed on the head's lower lip and it let out a choking sound.

"I guess not, then."

Trish offered a dry corner of its old familiar towel, and the head sucked greedily. How was this thing sustaining itself? She wondered if she might leave it here, happily sucking on the towel in the drawer for the day. But yesterday it was comforted when it was against her body. It liked to be against her body. And what if it let go of the towel? Stopped sucking as it slept and let the towel fall from its mouth. It's not like it could reach for it, pick it back up. She didn't want the thing to be distressed. And the noise. Ken and Anne.

Sure enough, the head began to cry as soon as the bus pulled into campus. What the hell was wrong with this thing? How did it know it was on campus, for one thing? The only place Trish felt comfortable was campus and this thing was ruining it. Or was it a matter of time? Did it need something around this time of day, maybe? What might the cyclical needs of a disembodied head be?

The hallway in the department was empty and Trish held the purse so it wouldn't bounce around and jogged to her office. As she came around the corner, she almost ran into Brandon standing outside her door.

She tried to laugh off her ridiculous state. "This thing won't stop crying."

Thank god someone knew about the head. Inside her office, she made a small show of relief at taking the crying purse from her shoulder and slowing her breathing. "Oh god, this thing."

Brandon tried a smile. He sat on the edge of the seat, hunched forward, his pack still on, hands in his pockets.

"Let's look at your manifolds, hey? It'll be good to stop thinking about…" Trish waved a hand at the shrieking purse on the filing cabinet.

Brandon shook his head. "No, I didn't come for that." He was still looking at the floor. He took a deep breath and glanced at Trish before he spoke to the floor. "I need to switch research groups and work with Xiu. I'm going to change supervisors."

A pressure set up in Trish's sternum, as though her chest was a vacuum. His ability to simply say what he needed. To rid himself of her. The ease with which he rendered her tenure application less tenable.

"No, Brandon. What? Why?"

He was staring at the floor again. "I'm sorry."

"Brandon, you can't just … I'm paying you."

"Dr. Martineau said he'd take care of it. He said he'd sort it out with you."

A new pressure filled Trish's head. "You talked to Martineau?"

"Yeah. Last night."

Sudden understanding sat Trish back in her chair. Brandon thought he could ditch her because of the head. Brandon thought the head rendered her less of a mathematician. Brandon thought the head compromised her mind, her authority. Her face filled with heat.

"Well, we'll see, Brandon. You can't just decide to change supervisors. It's not up to you. There's a process, which you have not followed."

Brandon nodded at the floor and then stood. "I'm sorry," he mumbled again and left without looking at her.

At least he knew to be ashamed.

After Brandon left, Trish snatched the head from the top of the filing cabinet and settled it in her lap. "Oh god, would you shut up."

And it did. Resting there in the crook of her crossed legs, its heat radiating through the leather of its purse, the cries stopped. Without lifting the weight of the head from her lap, she peered inside the bag. The little thing's entire face was wet and red. With a thumb and forefinger, and without touching the head, Trish nipped one of the cloths. The inside of the bag was warm and moist.

"Here." She held the bit of cloth out to the thing's mouth. Its lips brushed it and sucked it in. Like the suckers on an octopus's arm. Its eyes closed.

It was probably wisest to keep the purse over her shoulder for class. Bad enough to have to carry such a thing across campus. Completely ridiculous to wear it to give a lecture. A surefire way to draw attention to herself. Her collarbones vibrated with the knowledge that the whole class would notice.

Calculus 100—enormous and silent. Speak into an auditorium full of people and get absolutely no response. Not even a nodding head. Even Brandon and Miriam, who were required to attend for their TA assignment, sat and stared, giving her nothing back. It would have been less unnerving to speak into an empty room. At least then she would not have hoped for any response. As she spoke to their passive faces, she hated them. These kids obviously felt they were watching television, or a YouTube video, the passive consumers of some set of information that Trish was responsible for delivering to them. As if she'd failed at her job because she was not entertaining them. They were the failures—valuing entertainment over truth and beauty. As if they had a right to the love of her intellectual life, to the topic that had opened the world and made it glow for her. Their daddies paid to run her passion through their affectless faces, to render its beauty entirely dead and beside the point. At the front of the classroom, as she walked back and forth, spooling formulas across the whiteboard, Trish wondered why the students were there if they were so entirely uninterested. To please their bank-rolling daddies?

How do we let them vote, when they are too afraid to raise their hand and say they don't understand. If there was a topic about which anyone should be unafraid to express confusion, even ignorance, it should be university-level calculus. Yet never. They didn't understand; she saw the grades. Neither were the tutorial sessions Brandon and Miriam ran well-attended. It spoke to either their utter inability to express their ignorance, or worse, the inability to see that they did not understand. Did they make their way through the day thinking they understood? Making up some pretend logic to explain the subject matter, like children do?

When Trish turned away from the board, or stood at the lectern, the deep space of the night sky, replete with stars, cracked through her breastbone. She could protect the emptiness from the students' incurious and uncaring gaze with a hoodie or a thick sweater. But she could not teach like that. And a blouse could not cover the infinite hole in her chest, much less protect it from their bored gaze. First her love of math through the masher of their indifference and then the hole in her chest. If she wanted a research program these were her responsibilities: scrape the wonder of the universe into the garburator of the classroom; and let them gaze at the gaping black hole in her heart.

Today they could also peer into the gash of the purse strap across her chest. Well, it couldn't detract from her abilities as a scholar. If you couldn't discriminate against people for their gender or ability, you couldn't discriminate against them for the horrors that appeared to them.

She came through the doors at the bottom of the lecture hall and interrupted Brandon, who was whispering desperately to Miriam. He leaned over the arm of the desk to talk to her but had his face turned to the door that Trish always used. As soon as she came in, he jerked away from Miriam and stared at his shoes. Miriam smiled sympathetically. An ally. Remember to sign that form. Trish opened her lecture notes and asked if anyone had questions from their textbook readings. Of course, a person would need to have read the textbook to have questions and so there was only silence. "Then let's move on."

Trish was self-conscious about the purse hanging in front of her stomach as she faced the class and was relieved to turn away to write on the board. After several lines of formulae on the board, as she bent to write lower down, the purse hung further and further away from her body and began to sway in response to the movement of her arm. With a grunt of frustration she pulled the purse strap so that the head could rest on her back. Absurd to be seen to fuss with such a thing. Plus, now the whole class was staring at the purse behind her back.

When she finished on the bottom of the first board and moved to the top of the next, she took the opportunity to move the head to her front again. But then, when she turned to face the class to explain what she'd written, it was exposed again. She concentrated on looking casual and slowly slipped the strap so that the head hung behind her again. As she talked, she decided she would move the head to her front as she turned back to the board. This was a good idea. At least she would appear in control of the situation. Once she was at the board again with the head in front of her though, the very next line she needed to write was too low and the head hung away from her body, pulling on her neck. On the board she was working through a problem about the opening of a curve. That was an idea.

She turned to the class suddenly. "This is not working. Look…"

At the lectern, she pulled the purse strap over her head. Get the thing off. The strap tangled in her hair, leaving her struggling with her hand over her head. Finally, she threw the purse on top of her binder of lecture notes. The head banged against one of the metal rings and set up a holy lament. Trish buried her face in her hands. Brandon's eyes were wide and he glanced at Miriam, who was pushing herself back in her seat.

In the dark of her closed eyes, Trish decided she would just come clean. They needed to know. As their professor, she was a mentor—her students needed to benefit from her knowledge of the world. They needed her to show them that the world was a horror, a proving ground. She had survived and she could contribute to their lives in this way. It didn't have to be only math that she taught them. It would help them navigate the world.

"I know you're all wondering about this purse, and why I have it, and why it's crying. Well, I'll show you."

Brandon shook his head at her. But he was just a kid too. He wasn't a mentor, a guide.

She pinched the bottom corners of the purse and turned the whole thing over, spilling the crying head onto the paper in her binder.

"There! This is it! This is what is in the purse. I don't know what it is, and I don't know where it came from, or how, or why it came to me. But there it is. Satisfied?"

Miriam was the first to flee, her arms full of paper, her pack hanging from her left side. A buzz filled the room. Proof they could, in fact, talk.

"Does anyone have any questions?"

A few people, sitting on the aisles, stood, and left. At first it was merely a smattering. But there was soon consensus that class was dismissed. Brandon stayed in his seat, staring blankly, shaking his head.

A lone student made his way slowly down the risers. When he reached the bottom of the stairs he stopped and called to Trish, "Ma'am, will any of this be on the exam?"

The boy's voice brought Brandon back to the room and he stood and walked to the stairs. "No," he said, patting the kid on the back and indicating that they should leave together. "It won't be on the test."

Trish was alone with the sobbing head. At least she had some time now before her meeting with Tang.

Tang did not look up as Trish came into the office. Just stared at her monitor and typed. "Hi Trish. Take a seat. I just need to…" The sentence trailed off.

The head inside its purse wailed. Heat poured from the bag into Trish's belly. Was it because it was crying? Trish got hot when she cried. But the head was hot even when it was not crying. The agitation of the noise though. That made Trish hot.

Tang's brow furrowed and she turned to Trish, dropping her hands from their typing position. "You did not bring that thing with you?"

Trish started to cry. "I'm sorry. I have nothing else to do with it! I can't leave it crying at home alone."

"You can't bring it crying in here!"

"I'm sorry! I don't know what to do with it!" Trish sank into one of the chairs in front of Tang's desk. "Do you know what to do with it?" The plea shocked Trish. She had not intended to appeal to Tang. In fact, she had left the house determined to need no one, need no appeal. And why would anyone appeal to Tang?

"Let me see." Tang stretched her hand across the desk and flicked her fingers at the purse. "Thing's clamorous," she said to herself, her outstretched hand still waiting.

Handing the head to Tang was the edge of a darkness. Trish knew she had to step into the darkness, and that she and the head would pass through the moment. But she could not see through to the other side, could not calculate how the two of them and their entanglement might continue after. Nausea pushed into the soft space between her clavicles, and she struggled to pull the purse strap over her head. Amazed at the power of carbon to simply persist in the face of the impossible, Trish held the purse out to Tang. Her heart shook her entire body.

Tang snatched the purse from Trish's fingers and peered over its edge. Her head jerked back slightly. She sat back and took the purse with her so that it was right under her nose.

Trish wished she hadn't given Tang the purse. She had brought Tang with her into the abyss. It could only be ruin for her life as she knew it. Why had she even come to the meeting?

"I don't think I'm the person you should be talking to about this."

Now it was Trish's turn to jerk her head back in surprise.

"I'm very sorry, but I think you need to find a more appropriate outlet."

"I didn't come here for help with this! I came to talk about strategies for the next granting season."

"Well. You didn't come prepared." Tang placed the head on the desk but closer to herself, so that Trish would have to reach for it, which she didn't want to do for fear of suggesting she didn't trust Tang with the head.

Just then there was a knock at the door. Trish jumped and turned to the sound. Phillip Martineau, the current director of grad students in the department poked his head in through the door. "Oh! Trish. You're here."

"Are you looking for me?"

"No! No. I... um... Wei, could I see you when you're finished here, please?"

"Sure."

"How long?"

"We're almost finished."

They hadn't even started. The head squawked.

Martineau chuckled nervously. "Was that the thing? From the faculty meeting?"

Tang waved at the purse in front of her. "Yes, Trish brought it," her wave and tone morphed from dismissive to confused.

"Can I see it?" Martineau was already walking toward the desk. Without even looking at Trish, he leaned across her and snatched the purse from the desk, opened the flap and peered inside. His face opened in surprise and then closed in distaste. He closed the flap and tossed the purse back on the desk. "It's disgusting."

"Well, there's that," Tang agreed.

Martineau shook his head, indicating that he was finished with the topic. "If you could come to my office," he said from the door as he left.

"Yes. I need a minute," Tang assured him. Tang pushed the purse across the desk to Trish.

"We haven't talked about my applications."

"It doesn't seem like you're in a place to be thinking strategically at the moment. And even if we could think about strategy, you are hardly in a place to manage the responsibility."

"I'm here, aren't I? I showed up to work even with this thing."

"The judgement on that …"

"I need help with my grant applications! My tenure…"

"I don't think your career should be your concern right now. You clearly have larger matters to manage. Here…" Tang turned to the shelving unit behind her and began shuffling through stacks of paper. Finally, she let out an, "Ah." She turned and placed a bright yellow pamphlet on top of the purse. It was for campus health services. "Here," she tapped the pamphlet. "Why don't you check out counselling services. It's free. Maybe they can help."

"I'm not unwell, Tang. This thing just showed up. It happened to me."

Tang held out a palm to stop Trish. "I can't. Take this thing that has *happened to you*," she drew air quotes on either side of her face, "out of my office. When you've dealt with it, we can talk about your grant applications."

Remembering the troll from her childhood dream filled her belly with certainty—she was alone. Trish stood so quickly that the chair tipped over behind her. She ignored it and seized the head in its purse and the pamphlet in one hand and yanked her pack onto her back with the other. Down the hall, as she struggled to get her pack onto her back, she glanced into Martineau's office. Miriam was there. Normally, Trish would have stopped. Anything concerning her grad student was her responsibility. But she was too angry and just kept walking.

CHAPTER FIVE

Trish pushed out the building's heavy glass doors and squinted against the bright sun that shone down and reflected from the concrete pad outside the building. There were students playing frisbee on the grass, and people sat, alone or with others, under trees, or just in the middle of the lawn. If she were a normal person, she could just sit down on the grass somewhere. Try to enjoy herself. But how could she with this thing hanging from her neck? It would just cry and attract attention. No one else had gross, crying mysteries hanging from their necks. They laughed; they shared snacks and drank coffee. Trish did not even know where she was going for the moment, or why, or what she would do when she got there. She walked quickly down the sidewalk in the shade of the buildings lining the quad. The pamphlet for counselling services flapped as it swung in her hand. As she approached SUB she stopped and turned the pamphlet over. Yes, it was here in SUB. Maybe. Maybe she would just look in. Just see. At least it was a place to go—a direction in which to take herself. She folded the pamphlet and shoved it into her back pocket. No need for everyone in SUB to see where she was going. All the services were located upstairs in the building, but Trish had only ever been up there to access the pedway. At the top of the stairs, she followed wayfinding signs down a bright, wide hallway and then down a narrower one lined with closed doors.

Inside a door marked *Counselling Services* there was a small waiting area with a few chairs against the wall. A young man behind a desk at the end of the room raised his eyebrows and peered back at Trish.

"C'mon in," the man child said.

"Hi." Trish went through the door into the empty waiting room. "I didn't know…"

"Yes! Welcome." He leaned forward and folded his hands on the desk. "What can we do for you today?"

Through a gluey mouth Trish said, "I've never been here," then, "I'm faculty."

"Okay."

"How does this work?" She wanted to sit down. Drink some water.

"Well, I presume you want to see a counsellor?"

"I guess?" Far from the boy's desk, she lowered herself onto the corner of a chair.

"Let me just see if Preeta's free." He walked down a hall behind his desk, and Trish heard him whispering. Then he was beside his desk, beaming, holding an arm out in the direction from which he'd just come. "You're in luck! Preeta has some time right now."

A cylinder of metal ore ran from Trish's throat to her diaphragm. She doubted very much that she was in luck. "Oh. I don't…"

"Come." The kid smiled kindly, waved her toward him, and began to walk, his arm still pointing in the direction he was walking. The head in its purse banged rhythmically against Trish's stomach as she followed.

The boy stopped and turned with a flourish on the far side of an open door. "Please."

What were they so eager about around here? Would she be invited to drink Kool-Aid? She turned cautiously to look through the door. A slim Indian woman in a fitted black skirt with a flair at the bottom and 1940s-style heels, tied with ribbons, stood looking down at paper on a desk. Her hair was cut in long layers so that it bounced and swung as she looked over to Trish. Deep purple lipstick. She wore a faded blue jean jacket, and on the chair behind her sat a large satchel of the trendy fake-and-really-not-cheap leather.

"I'll leave you to it." The receptionist skipped away, lightly touching Trish's shoulder as he passed.

"Hi." The woman sounded like it was a relief to see Trish.

"I'm sorry," Trish gestured back to the boy. "I just…"

"No. It's great." Preeta closed the door. "I'm glad it worked out this way." She threw a blanket off a chair and gestured to it. A small fountain of rocks and recycled water burbled quietly on the table beside the chair. "Have a seat."

Trish did not want to sit and get this lovely woman's office all dirty. But Preeta sat, and Trish could hardly just stand over the woman. At the edge of the seat, she tried to look in control.

"Please, make yourself comfortable. You can hang your purse on the rack."

"No, no, that's fine," Trish snorted. Then she found she was laughing. "You really don't want that."

Preeta smiled. "Okay. You hold onto it if you like." Preeta sat back in her chair, crossed her legs, and folded her hands in her lap, like she could sit there smiling all day. "So, what brings you in today?"

"Me? Oh. No. I just… He just…" Trish gestured to the door to indicate that the kindly boy had forced her in.

Preeta smiled, "Yes, but what made you even open our door?"

Suddenly, as if a steam valve opened in her guts, Trish needed out of her coat and pack and the purse. She dropped everything on the floor beside her and was surprised to find she was in her teaching clothes. It seemed like class was several days ago. The front of her shirt looked like she'd been wearing it for several days, too. "I don't really know. My chair suggested I come here. This thing has happened, and it doesn't have anything to do with my work but everyone's very distressed by it and so they're making it about my work. Everyone else. Not me. I just want to work, you know? I don't see what it has to do with work but they're all so distressed by it. I don't know. They're the ones who keep making it about work."

Preeta nodded slowly. "It sounds as though your colleagues are not giving you the support you need right now. Where do you work?"

"Math. I'm in math. I don't need support. Not from them."

"I see. So, there is something you want help with but you're not expecting it to come from them. What do you study?"

"Right! And they say I'm asking too much of them! I study geometry. Geometry of dimensions higher than four."

"*Higher* than four? I can't imagine that."

"That's one of the debates, yes. Can we transfer the sensual experience of three-dimensional space to higher dimensions? Curved spaces, too. We use a lot of visual proofs."

Preeta shook her head. "That's incredible. Alright. So, what's happened that you're looking for support?"

"Oh. You really don't want to know."

"Try me."

"Something weird."

"Something distressing has happened."

"Yes. Yes. Yeah, it's distressing."

"What's happened?"

"I'm worried you won't believe me. But can I show you?"

"You don't have to show me. I'll believe you."

Trish imagined showing this woman the head. It was not a black void; she could see the continuity. She did not know how Preeta would respond, but she could see that they would continue to exist together in the room with the sound of the water trickling quietly in her fountain. "This head. This disembodied head. It's just a head. It's a little baby head. But it's not like severed or anything. It's alive. It's just a little, self-contained head. It just arrived on my dresser yesterday morning."

Preeta's chin rose, and she nodded as if she understood entirely, as if she'd even expected it. Maybe she was in on it. "The arrival of a disembodied head would certainly be distressing. I'd like to ask you a few questions. Just to ensure your safety. Would that be alright?"

Trish bit her lip and shrugged.

"Do you think anyone left the head there?"

Trish shook her head.

"Was anything taken?"

Again.

"And you haven't noticed anything else strange?"

"No!"

Preeta nodded. "Great. Okay. So you don't know where the head came from but you're pretty sure you're not in any immediate physical danger?"

"I feel like there's danger everywhere."

"Right. But you don't think, for example, that someone's hiding and waiting to pounce on you?"

How they could discount the possibility, Trish did not know. But clearly this woman did not want Trish to think there was anyone waiting to pounce, and she had taken the time to see her. "No."

"Can I... is that the head in there?" Preeta pointed at the purse with an outstretched hand.

Trish did not want to subject the poor woman to such a thing. But who was she to think she knew better what was good for her? She held the purse up from her lap, barely extending her arm. When Preeta took the purse, Trish's hand fell into her lap, and she stared at it.

"Well, this little thing is just tender, isn't it?" Preeta was staring down into the purse. "It's fairly extraordinary. Look at its little eyelashes. How is it breathing?" At this, Preeta held the purse at eye level and examined its bottom and back.

Trish shook her head to clear the impossible image.

"Can I hold it?"

Trish wanted to go to sleep. She shrugged and slouched back in the chair. The ceiling panel above Preeta's window was stained brown with moisture. The little head clicked its tongue.

"Oh, it's really delicate." Preeta looked across at Trish as if she was asking her mother for a puppy.

Trish shook her head at the ceiling. "I haven't looked at it that closely."

Now Preeta sat back, cradling the head against her body. Maybe she would keep it? Trish wanted to lurch forward and insist on it, but knew she'd better bide her time and so simply sat back in the chair. As she waited, she searched the ceiling tiles for a pattern so she could put numbers on it.

Around the time the troll came to her room, Trish became aware that some kids in her grade two class went for extra help in math and reading. There was even a little room dedicated to this extra help. She was jealous and decided to ask for help with math so that she could go to the room, too. The tutor was someone's grandmother, a retired teacher. The woman had soft grey curls and old-fashioned brown shoes. She gave

Trish a sheet of addition and subtraction problems and gave the paper a little pat. Trish agreed with the little pat; it was exciting. She solved the problems and looked at the woman for the next sheet. The grandmother was looking at a sheet inside a file folder.

"I thought you were in grade two?"

Trish nodded.

"These weren't hard for you?"

"I love them!" Witless to show her hand like that.

The chairs in the room were not kid-sized like the chairs in her classroom. She crossed her ankles and swung her legs, eyeing the stack of paper at the woman's left hand.

"Try this." The grandmother pushed a page filled with lines of numbers across the table. The idea was to count in patterns.

"These are really fun," Trish assured the woman, and drew careful arcs to show the patterns.

"Do you know how to multiply?"

"What's that?"

"It's counting by patterns."

"Same as this."

The woman nodded and put a page of single digit multiplier problems in front of Trish and pointed to the first question. "This means two groups of ten."

"Twenty," Trish flourished the tale of the two.

"Yes. What does this one mean?"

"Four groups of five. Can multiplication be different questions?"

The woman's grey curls bobbed. "Look at this one."

The numbers appeared like clouds in Trish's mind's eye and she scrambled up and over them, their buoyancy holding her aloft no matter how hard she landed on them.

"Three groups of six. Eighteen. Can I keep going?"

Trish filled the rows, concentrating on making her numbers neat to impress the grandmother. When she finished that sheet, the woman showed her how to carry products across place value and Trish felt like she was rushing down a slide.

"It seems like you don't need help with math. It seems like you need some harder math to do in school. Would you like that?"

"I like it here, though." Trish looked around the room, the metal of the grown-up chair cool against her palms.

"Maybe we can take some time together occasionally."

That night, Trish's mother told her that the school had called and asked if Trish might be avoiding going home. With a jittery fury, her mother yelled, "I can't believe you didn't think about how your little stunt would make me look! Grow up."

Beside Deidre, Trish's father snorted and shook his head.

The next day, Trish's teacher gave her a grade four math book, and she worked through that by herself during the daily math lesson. She tore the pages along their perforated edges to take home and work on in the evenings. But she never set foot in the tutoring room again.

When she realized she'd been quiet for too long, Trish sat up suddenly.

"Take your time," Preeta smiled. "Come back slowly."

Trish slowed her movements to comply.

"What are you feeling now?"

Wasn't the question, *how are you feeling*?

"Fine, I guess. A bit calmer."

Preeta nodded and kept smiling, as though she was proud of Trish for being calm.

"It helps to have someone share the weight."

Trish only nodded. She figured she should take the head back from Preeta.

"How do you think you'll proceed?"

"I have no idea. I just want to live my life. I just want to… I don't know… keep going."

"I can certainly understand that urge."

"I can't believe how resistant everyone is. How they judge me for this thing!"

"It's a new reality. You weren't ready for it. They weren't ready for it."

"You think they'll be better after a while?"

Preeta sniffed and shook her head. "You'll learn to integrate this new reality. You will integrate it."

"I feel like *the world* cannot integrate it." Trish panned an open palm around the room.

"I expect that you will need to incorporate the head into your understanding. You will need to change."

"I don't want to."

"Right, yes. But you don't need to be there yet. You're just beginning. Just touch the edge of it."

"The head?"

"No. But that's a good question. Have you touched the head?"

Trish's lips curled.

"That's okay. What I meant was to just touch the edge of the reality. Just accept what's here now. The terror and the head. Both. Right now, it's new and you're afraid and that's okay."

"How? How is it okay?"

"It's okay to be afraid. You don't have to move past that to a solution."

"I'd really like a solution."

"You're a math professor. You understand that problems take time. You're being too hard on yourself."

"How am I being hard on myself? This horror showed up and I don't know what it is or where it came from or what it means. I'm not blaming myself. I just want to figure it out."

"I hear that. When you move too fast with it though, you're overwhelmed. You panic because you don't have a solution."

That made a bit of sense. "You're proposing that I treat the head like a math problem?"

"Let's try." Preeta spread her palms open in front of her as though showing Trish a display of hors d'oeuvres. "How would you approach a math problem?"

"I'd start with what I already knew—variables I understood. There's nothing about this head that I understand."

"That's too fast already. Let's stay away from the head for a minute and just look at some of the variables surrounding the head. What do you know for sure? Not about the head. Just anything."

"Just anything? Well, this thing is ruining my career!"

"Slower still. When did you find the head?"

"I told you. Yesterday. My birthday."

Preeta's eyes went wide, and the corners of her mouth turned down. She nodded slowly.

"It was your birthday." She said this as if she was talking to herself. "Happy belated birthday."

Trish raised her eyebrows. By that logic, every introduction should be met with belated birthday wishes.

"What did you do once you found it?"

"I panicked." Trish made her eyes wide and looked at Preeta to indicate that this was the reasonable extent of anyone's reaction. But Preeta just waited. "I needed to get dressed, which was quite the task, since the thing was on my dresser."

"You were not dressed?"

"It wasn't there when I woke up. And then I heard it crying while I was in the shower. I thought there was a leak in the building or something. But it was this thing crying on my dresser! I had to deal with it in order to even get ready to deal with it, you know?"

"Yes, you had to make yourself more vulnerable in order to make yourself less vulnerable."

"Right." Trish just wanted to get through the rest of the story. "I grabbed my clothes and ran back to the bathroom and called my friend Luca. I just wanted someone there with me. Thank God my father wasn't there."

Preeta's forehead wrinkled, and she shook her head. "Why would your father be there? Does he live with you?"

"No, no. I don't know why I said that."

"But you thought it?"

"It just came and went."

"Okay. Can we try something? I have an idea. Can we try something?"

What could they possibly do?

"Lean back in the chair. Try to relax. Close your eyes."

Trish did as she was told.

"No need to squeeze your eyes shut. Just close them lightly."

Trish tried to relax her face.

"Alright. Now, we're going to slow down the moment when you first found the head."

Trish's eyes popped open.

"It's okay, you're here. Not there. Nothing bad will happen."

She closed her eyes again.

"Don't start imagining yet. Stay here in the room. The point is to slow down the moment so that you can re-do it. So that you can have some control over the encounter this time. Does that make sense?"

Trish raised her eyebrows and wobbled her head in consideration. She could not deny the internal logic of the idea.

"For example: Maybe this time when you see the head, you have a friend with you. Or maybe this time when you see the head, you're already dressed and so feel a bit safer."

"What if something even worse turns up this time?"

"No, no. It's only exactly what happened with the changes you would like to make. Whatever you would like to have happened."

"I guess a friend would be good."

"Okay, good. Imagine the moment again. You're there and you see the head. Who's there with you?"

"I wanted Luca."

"Okay, so Luca's there?"

"Yes."

"Alright, so now I want you to just feel the sensation of finding the head with Luca there. How is it different from finding the head all alone?"

"It's easier. It's not as scary. It's still scary and confusing but I'm relieved that we're together."

"Right. You can share the shock a bit."

"I guess. It's also almost like it's a thing we have in common. It's something we share." Suddenly Trish was looking at Preeta. "That's a bit ridiculous—wanting my friend to be exposed to this horror so that we have something in common. What's wrong with me?"

"No, no. You're not wishing bad things on your friend. You're wishing a friend for your own hard experience."

"Well, it's a bit selfish."

"Was Luca helpful?"

"In reality?"

Preeta nodded.

"What can I expect—dragging around this monstrosity."

"Do you have any other friends you can call on for support?"

Trish squinted at her. "No! This thing is ridiculous. Awful. Humiliating."

"But you called Luca?"

"Luca's different."

"No one else is as close as Luca?"

"I mean, I have my mother, though she's a bit of a problem these days. And I have my friend Jess. But I don't want to bother her! I don't see how anyone can just accept… I want someone to accept this just because they love me. But it's too embarrassing."

"Trish, listen. I don't think work is a great place for you right now. I know your work has been a sort of refuge for you. But now that this head has arrived… Look, professors have sick leave. Take some time off to figure out what to do with this head. Learn how to live with it, maybe. At least let the horror calm down. The university is not built to absorb shock and horror."

She gave a snort of laughter.

"Sometimes it creates shock and horror."

"Wait. Do you think the university caused the head?" Maybe they were getting somewhere.

"No. I'm sorry. I was being flippant. Trish, look, you're going to need to imagine new solutions for yourself. Remember how it felt to imagine a friend with you when you discovered the head?"

Trish nodded, guilt-ridden.

"It's a new reality you'll need to integrate into your life. You'll need to begin to occupy the world differently now."

That's when Trish understood. This woman didn't want Trish to succeed in her career either. Give up on what you love, she was saying. Well, too bad. Trish would not abandon herself.

Back in the sunshine outside SUB, Trish remembered the stack of CVs and Miriam's form sitting on her desk. See—there was work to do! The purse was heavy, and the strap stuck to Trish's neck. All she needed was to get the pile of paper and then she could get on the bus back home.

As Trish opened her office door, Tang appeared beside her, and behind her Martineau was leaving Anderson's office, laughing, and saying thanks and goodbye. He came and stood beside Tang, his hands shoved in his pockets.

"We need to talk to you."

Trish looked back at Anderson's door. "You ambushed me?"

"We need to talk."

Trish opened the door and let them in but did not invite them to sit. She began to gather the stack of paper on her desk. "I don't really have time, Tang. I'm taking these CVs home to read." The weight of the head pulled the purse away from her body as she leaned over the desk to gather the papers.

"We've had reports from your grad students about inappropriate behaviour," Martineau chimed in.

The head bumped against Trish's belly as she stood and threw her hands in the air. All she wanted was to get on with her life, take these CVs home to review. It's not like it was work she wanted to do, this was work that needed to be done in order to keep her job. And now she wasn't even going to be allowed to do that. "What are you talking about?!"

"You've scared Miriam quite badly and Brandon too is deeply uncomfortable. They have both written formal complaints against you."

"What? When did I scare them? How did I scare them?"

Martineau held his palms out. "Unfortunately, I can't discuss the details of the students' complaints."

Brandon had betrayed her. They had a rapport, an under-standing. He was her student. He was supposed to trust her —to let her be someone he trusted.

"You've scared them both with the head," Tang lowered her voice to indicate discretion.

Martineau gazed at the floor and hunched his shoulders.

"The head is not me! I'm just doing my best under the circumstances."

"Why would you show them this head?! You've undermined their confidence in you. What did you think would happen? You can't expect people—students!—to take you seriously with this monstrosity flapping around in front of you!"

"What does this thing have to do with anyone's confidence in me as a professor?"

"Look. Maybe it's not right. But it's the way it is. You can't reveal horrifying things to students and expect them to maintain the same respect for you. You compromise your own authority. The university considers this kind of thing dangerous."

This is what Preeta had said. "Ha. The university creates this kind of thing!"

Tang shook her head angrily. Martineau's eyes went wide but he didn't move, just kept staring at the floor. "What are you talking about, Trish? No."

Trish cocked an eyebrow and shrugged.

"Phillip ..." Tang passed the ball to Martineau.

"I've spoken to Brandon and Miriam and I've also talked to senior administration in the faculty. The next step in the complaint procedure is for *you* to meet with them at the faculty, to tell your side of the story."

Tang interrupted, "Your side of the story could be strength-ened significantly if…" She trailed off, a pop of air came from her chest and she looked around the room frantically. "Trish, why have you not gone to the police with this thing?"

"The police? What? No. No, no, no. It's too degrading. No."

"But you're willing to parade it around in front of your students?"

Trish had never liked Martineau. There was something off. He wasn't trustworthy. "I did not parade it around. But doesn't that just prove my point? Brandon and Miriam are my students. And look how they reacted to this thing."

"People could take you more seriously if you went to the police. It would be a demonstration of... of your good faith."

"Good faith in what?"

"Not good faith. What's the word I'm looking for?" Tang turned to Martineau as if the German with the French name might have a larger English vocabulary than she did.

"Innocence?" he offered.

"Yes! Innocence. If you went to the police, it would be a demonstration of your innocence. It would show the university your commitment to your innocence."

"The police could legitimize this, is what you're saying?"

Tang smiled and nodded eagerly. "Exactly."

Trish shook her head.

Martineau took a hand from his pocket and held it up. "Okay, look, if you go to the police, it will help your case. But, you can also take some time away."

"Away? What?"

"You've behaved inappropriately and upset students. But Brandon and Miriam don't want to see you in trouble. In the complaint procedure there is also a loop... a mechanism... that pauses the process if you take time away from the university. It's a kind of cooling off period. Gives everyone a chance to think. Re-evaluate."

"Maybe go to the police?" Tang suggested.

"Miriam and Brandon are happy to proceed this way."

"A leave?"

"Yes, for the remainder of the semester at least but longer can be arranged."

"What? But my grant applications."

"We can pause your tenure process and then the grant applications can wait."

"No. What? I see what happens to women who pause the tenure process. Everyone knows pausing the tenure clock is a sign of weakness. An admission of defeat."

"Well." Tang held out her hands to demonstrate that this was simply where they were. "If you do not take the leave, effective immediately, the formal complaint process will simply go ahead. You will, in all likelihood, receive a formal reprimand and be placed on probation."

Martineau shoved his hands back into his pockets.

"Probation?"

"You don't have tenure, Trish. See—the police could help." Tang spoke as if Trish were a tired child at the end of a long day at the fair.

"Your tenure clock would restart after the probation period is complete," Martineau explained.

Trish felt like she had tipped too far back in her chair. "Why am I being punished for this horror that is not my fault?!"

"You're not being punished, Trish. We're trying to maintain a standard of propriety here at the university."

"I am not doing anything improper! This thing has just come to me."

"We believe you." Tang turned to Martineau for confirmation, her hand on her heart.

He nodded as though expressing willingness to eat meat from a department store diner.

"I'm trying to make my way with it as best as I can."

"You can't bring it here. It doesn't belong here."

"Trish, look, you obviously don't have the whole story about this head. If you take the time off, you can go to the police…"

"I'm not going to the police!"

"Whatever, fine. You can use the time to find out what the real story is. Get to the truth of this thing." Did Tang know something? The troll. There was nowhere to turn.

"Fine."

"Good."

Martineau handed Tang a file folder he had clutched between his chest and his arm. "You only need to sign here." Tang placed the folder on Trish's desk and pointed to a line that was already highlighted.

As Trish signed, Tang said, "In taking this leave, you elect to accept fifty percent of your salary."

The pen froze. But it was too late. Her signature was complete. She shoved the paper across the desk at Tang, who handed it over to Martineau. Trish gathered the stack of CVs.

"You won't need those."

Martineau snorted and opened the door.

Tang looked back over her shoulder at Trish from the doorway. "You're relieved of your administrative duties as well."

And then they were gone.

The HVAC system whooshed quietly. Trish pulled the purse over her head and felt immediate relief from its weight. But as soon as she put the purse down on the desk, the head started to cry. Trish grasped fistfuls of hair in both hands and pulled. "Oh god, shut up, shut up, shut up," she whispered through clenched teeth.

It did not shut up.

Well, they couldn't stop her from thinking—her actual work. She took the stack of journal articles from her desk and a couple of books from her shelf. She didn't take the time to put them in her pack, just gathered everything in her arms, the purse strap clutched in a fist, the empty pack on one shoulder. Down the hall, she saw Tang and Martineau whispering. When they saw her, they stood up straight and went in separate directions. Understanding seized Trish's heart and burned her gut—impossible to find safety at the university. Maybe that's what the head was here for? Was it warning her? Protecting her?

Once, after a Saturday math competition, Trish walked out of the school to find her father standing in the parking lot waiting for her, arms crossed tightly. It was supposed to be her mother who picked her up.

"How'd you do?" He uncrossed his arms and pulled the keys out of his coat pocket.

Trish held up the small trophy she had earned.

"Gee. Impressive." He rolled his eyes. "Good thing we paid twenty dollars for that." He held her cheeks tightly and kissed her on the lips as the car keys pressed into her jaw.

A neighbour had needed her mother—"lady problems"—and so her father had come instead. Trish was shocked to think that her mother considered this a viable solution.

CHAPTER SIX

Now, on the bus, Trish sat immediately in the front seats for people with limited mobility. Once she was settled, she cooed into the purse to keep the head quiet, and no one told her to move. The humiliation of the meeting with Tang and Martineau burned. They had probably told the entire department by now.

Trish decided to study math at university after she saw the movie *Cube* at a classmate's house with a bunch of people. She sat beside the class Casanova with a blanket over her legs so that he could put his hand down her pants while they watched. This did not signal that Trish was special. The boy put his hand down everyone's pants. He had once fingered Trish's friend, May, in the local swimming pool—put his hand under her suit between her legs. The idea of May's vagina exposed to pool water scared Trish. But really, a bathing suit wasn't much protection either. All the girls were probably stupid to go swimming and expose themselves to the dirty water. Another time, in the dark hallway leading to the bathroom at a bowling alley, the boy had made Trish pull on his penis, which was slick and soon coated with small rolls of dead skin. Watching *Cube* with this boy's hand in her pants was inconvenient and unpleasant but at least she didn't have to touch his sweaty penis.

In the movie, a group of strangers all named after prisons, are trapped in a system of moving rooms, some deadly, others not, promising always threat or escape. A young woman in the group, Leaven, is a mathematician and uses numbers engraved on the doors to determine whether the rooms are safe, as well as the limits of the system and an escape route. When Leaven figures out she can use the numbers as Cartesian coordinates, Trish, in her excitement whispered, "Oh, wow."

Beside her on the couch, the boy gave a little snort of laughter and wrenched his hand out of her pants. The yank on her hips and the cold he left behind startled Trish back to the room and she looked over at him.

Smug, he leaned over and whispered into her ear, "Glad you liked it."

Pretty soon the boy got up, joked around with another boy in the room, and then left with his arm around another girl. Trish tucked her legs up, pulled the blanket up to her chin and turned her attention back to the movie. That was it; math needed to be taken seriously.

She sagged off the bus. On the three-block walk to her house, Trish saw women everywhere in puffy vests and knee-high boots, hands shoved deep into their pockets, nothing hanging off their bodies. Maybe a dog on a leash. A thing with legs at least. And here Trish came at them, sweaty, out of breath, with a mass of flesh hanging from her neck.

At home, she walked straight through her apartment to the kitchen and dropped her pack on the floor and the stack of papers and books on the table. The real relief came when she got the purse off her shoulder. Enough was enough. It was time to figure this thing out. Take the matter in hand and really look at it closely.

Preeta's idea to *touch the edge of it* seemed sensible. You could determine a lot with just an edge. Trish fetched the rubber dish gloves from under the kitchen sink. Soft, warm air came to her nose as she peered past the neon yellow to the head inside the purse, and she felt a sudden tenderness for the thing. She swirled a dish towel on the table in front of her and reached into the purse. But as soon as she touched the head, it started to squawk. All she needed to do was get it out of the purse and onto the towel where it would be comfortable. But she couldn't lever her hand under it, just kept pushing it over. Using both hands would work but then she couldn't hold the purse open to see. The rubber of the gloves stuck and vibrated against the head's skin. The sting of having one hair pulled. The head continued to cry.

"Alright, alright!"

Trish peeled the gloves off and reached into the purse with bare hands, eyes squeezed shut. But the thing did not complain. It was soft, smooth, and slightly squishy. Warm air brushed Trish's wrists, like when you practice kissing on your own arm. Moving quickly, she placed the head on the towel, sat up straighter and stared down at it.

Its skin colour was not unappealing—a creamy white with maybe a golden undertone—though its cheeks were a splotchy red like the pink of a peach's dark patch. Beyond the puckers around its bottom edge, the thing was unblemished. The puckers must be how it was closed off from where its body should be. But there was no line like a scar. How was this thing processing oxygen? Trish pushed a thumb up into the chin. It yielded but there was bone there, giving it form. She traced a finger back along its jaw, which stopped where a normal jaw stops. Behind that the skin just gave more until the skull started. The bottom of the head behind the jaw yielded to pressure. It was only covered with skin. Trish pushed the pad of her thumb in until the very edge of her nail. The thing cried out.

"Sssh. Sorry, sorry. I'll stop."

She had not meant to hurt it and began to smooth its hair and straighten its eyebrows to quiet it. There were tiny hairs over the top and back of its head and it had translucent eyebrows and minuscule eyelashes over deep blue eyes. For a while she'd been sleeping with a guy who had sailed all over the world. He liked pain, that guy, and Trish bought a pin tool for his balls, which she still had because, even though it wasn't any loss when he left, the pins would pierce the garbage bag, so how was she supposed to get rid of it? He said there was a shade of blue that exists only in the deepest oceans. Trish imagined she was seeing that colour now.

On the Monday after she saw *Cube*, Trish took her time packing up her books after math class and walked to the front of the room as everyone else poured out. The teacher, Mr. Rose, was at the whiteboard, wiping it down. His body twisted side-to-side with the effort.

"I'd like to do some extra work."

Mr. Rose put the eraser down on the table in front of him and nodded, "Yes, alright."

He organized readings for her and found websites for her to investigate and gave her problems to work on outside of class. "Let me know if you have questions."

The determination to study math was a force that felt beyond Trish, as though it acted through her. So she was grateful to Mr. Rose, and utterly lost about what he expected from her. When she interacted with boys of any age or relation to her—the next-door neighbour, a friend's younger brother, the nerdy kid at school she'd known since infancy, the boys on the football team—she presumed it was her responsibility to summon and then express sexual interest in them, and then to serve their desire for her as it emerged. When she was in grade school, this meant letting Billy Smiley touch her *down there* after school behind the dumpsters at 7-11 while he told her about how his older brother had recently bitten off a girl's "pussy" and spit the bloody flesh all over the wall beside the bed. That night, Trish asked her mother if she too had a pussy and was told not to be disgusting.

And of course, Trish and all her friends had been letting the high school tough guy put his hands down their pants in public since grade seven. Even though she knew it was happening with other girls and felt awful for them, Trish pretended that she was convinced no one else knew it was happening to her or was embarrassed for her. In high school, Trish's responsibility to boys extended to include lots of sex at house parties in unfamiliar neighbourhoods, with boys she'd never met and never saw again, sometimes more than one boy in a night. Once, one of them dug a golf club out of a pile of clothes and sporting equipment on the floor of the closet in the room they were in and used that to fuck her.

But Mr. Rose was a teacher. That fact made Trish nervous about offering this kind of attention. It was at once her responsibility to men, and bad behaviour on her part. Besides, why on earth would he want her? Also, she felt sad at the thought of having sex with him, which confused her. Why would she feel anything about having sex with someone? But she really wanted the work. An image of Leaven in *Cube* floated in her mind's eye—the couple of times the character smiled. Did she want the work badly enough to have the sex? Yes, ultimately, she did. It would be worth it and how bad could it be? She could get used to it. She had not wanted to let Billy Smiley touch her either. But everything after that had been easier. In fact, maybe this was just the next step to adulthood. She would have the math and the maturity.

Still, to delay the inevitable, Trish tried to contain her excitement about the work. But Mr. Rose's enthusiasm mirrored her own and soon problems were "cool," and solutions were "amazing." Unwittingly, Trish one day confessed to Mr. Rose that she loved math because it was the power to model physical problems.

He nodded eagerly, adding, "And make predictions!"

Trish felt understood in a way she never had before, which only deepened her regret and disappointment about the pending sexual encounter. She didn't want to let him touch her. It was always so cold. So much nicer to be at her desk with the heat of the lamp on her neck, or under the blankets with her books and her calculator, modelling physical problems with numbers.

About a month into the work with Mr. Rose, Trish found a problem for which she could not find the solution. The question was about a circular cam, with a rod touching its edge. The wheel rotated around a pin at its outside edge, so that it moved away from and then toward the rod, which moved in and out on a spring. The problem was to solve for the velocity and acceleration of the rod when the wheel was at such a point that the angle made by the line of the rod across the bottom of the cam and a straight line from the rod's point to the centre was thirty degrees. Trish measured the various coordinates from the fixed point and related them to each other using trigonometry. It had taken her about an hour but now she was on firm footing. Since $OC = BC = r \cos \emptyset$, then $x = 2r \cos \emptyset$.

But she could not see how to move from this solution for the angle and distance to the analysis of the rod's acceleration and velocity. The solution required a statement of time. Where the rod touched the cam depended on it having rotated there, which would have taken time. She tried presuming different points on the cam and bringing them into relation through other trig formulas. But without information about the time variable, she still could not determine velocity or acceleration. And there was no information about time in the question. The tickle in her back would not be eased no matter how straight she sat, so she put the problem aside and went for a run.

During math on Monday, she took the problem out once more, hoping that her subconscious had figured it out overnight. But the problem did not yield. After the bell rang and everyone left, she took it to Mr. Rose. The paper fluttered in her hand as she jerked down each riser.

"I can't…" She pushed the paper over to Mr. Rose, so frustrated she nearly cried.

He read the problem, scraping his fingernails up the five o'clock shadow on his neck. Then, without speaking, he took the page of work and read through what she'd done.

"No," he said.

Trish's heart sank. Even what she thought she had was wrong.

Mr. Rose walked to a row of books he kept behind his desk. "You can't. You need the chain rule. The chain rule will let you get the time derivative." He flipped through chunks of a thick textbook. "Here," he turned the book to Trish and pointed to a series of formulas. "The chain rule."

Trish stared down at them. It was calculus. The simplicity of the solution stunned her. "It's just turn-the-handle math."

"I know," Mr. Rose waved a hand in the air as if making a proclamation.

Trish still couldn't believe it. "Should I not have been able to figure this out on my own?"

"No, no," Mr. Rose waved away the suggestion. "Maybe once you're in your PhD."

She looked back down at the book, took the paper back from Mr. Rose and started to work. After the first two steps of the chain rule, she was suddenly aware that she was not paying any attention to Mr. Rose. Just standing there absorbed in her work. She stood up from the book.

"Trish, it's really impressive"—he was nodding his head, his eyebrows raised—"that you got as far as you did. You have a fierce intelligence. I hope you know that."

Trish had been at the height of the cam's rotation. And now she started to fall. It was time. The nature of a circle, always both up and down.

His left hand rested on the desk, curled slightly beside the textbook, the evenly trimmed nails, the blue veins across the top. She reached over and then her own hand was on top of his. Her thumb stroked, but did not feel, the ridges of his index finger. Mr. Rose jolted like the fire alarm had gone off and Trish's hand thudded to the table.

"I'm sorry!" Humiliation coursed into her face.

"No. Trish, I'm sorry. I didn't... Listen, it's just... I'm your teacher. It's not appropriate that we have any physical contact."

"Of course. I'm sorry. I'm sorry. I'm sorry." Using the refrain like a gravitational wave, she hoped to wind back time or move herself from that place. A roar filled her head. She seized her calculator from the table and threw it into her open pack, followed by her binder and textbook.

Out in the empty parking lot, grey clouds bulged with

rain. A whimper in her throat surprised Trish. She heard her name. Mr. Rose was walking toward her from the school doors. And Trish ran.

Her pack beat against her lower back. She held the straps tightly, forced her strides longer until she could feel her hip flexors stretch and her calf muscles pull. She exhaled hard and counted seven or eight strides before she let herself take in another breath. Metal at the back of her mouth as her lungs desperately seized air. Past the street she needed to get home, she stopped recognizing landmarks. Still she ran.

A pain like the snap of an elastic band shot through her calf. She yelped like a puppy and came to a hopping stop. To her right was a field with a gully of trees. Maybe she could get lost in there. She limped into the gully, dropped her pack, and dove to the earth. The hard ground drove sharp rocks and twigs into and along her palms. She took handfuls of the stuff and scraped it up and down her face, her skin tearing open. She pounded her fists into her thighs, over and over, pressed into them with all her strength and, stretching her neck, screamed noiselessly into the trees, her eyes wide. Small squeaks escaped her throat. Her whole body shook with the effort. Again and again, she screamed silently to the trees. Her head would not stop its colossal roar though she pounded it with her fists. She looked at the trees and wanted to smash her temple into a broken branch. But she knew she could not. The destruction would be too great.

A destruction too great. God, her calculator. She crawled back through the detritus to her pack. Her fingers would not work. They nipped and dropped and scratched at the fabric until she could finally clutch the pull and tug the zipper open. The teeth of the zipper scraped the back of her hand as she reached inside.

She flipped open the soft rubber cover, but the calculator did not turn on. Through the trees around her, the light was fading. At the edge of the grove she tried the power button again. The screen lit, filled with random numbers. As she pressed the soft button to clear the screen, she held her breath. A zero. For the time it took the relief to rush through her body, she felt nothing but gratitude. She ran a few formulas to be sure, and then took the calculator back to where she had been and sat with it in her lap. Her heart thumped in her ears and after a while she felt its beat rocking her. Soon she grew cold.

At home she went straight upstairs to wash the mud off her face. The white of her right eye had a splotch of red in it, the skin around her temple was scratched.

At dinner her mother asked, "What happened to your eye?"

Trish kept her head down.

"Gym."

"Well, Jesus, be more careful. People are going to think we're hitting you."

The head let out a small whimper and Trish jerked backward, surprised to find herself so absorbed in the thing. It was late afternoon. Trish needed something to do.

"Maybe we should go to the beach."

The head clicked its tongue.

The bin of hats and scarves was still on the floor from the day before. Trish dug through and found an old fanny pack. Lined with a tea towel, it could be cozy for the head. With the flap unzipped, the head would get some nice air and sun. When she needed to, she could zip it away so no one could see.

At the water, she walked along the sidewalk above the beach, and then stopped and leaned against the concrete wall, looking out over the surf. The crowd gave the place a carnival atmosphere, and small children splashed in the waves. Now that she had touched the head, she wanted to hold it again. It was soft. Warm. She took the head out of the fanny pack and held it out in the sun. Its skin gave slightly under the pressure of her fingers, which was satisfying. It closed its eyes as she stroked its side with a finger. The sun lit the tiny hairs on its face, and it seemed to glow.

"What have you born, sister?"

A white guy on roller blades, his hair in dreadlocks, so close Trish could feel the heat radiating from his body. A guitar was slung across his back with a strap woven in colours and patterns meant to indicate Central America but produced en masse in China by child labour.

He looked her in the eye. "I see your power." He held his hand out over the head, "This is a potent icon."

Trish opened her mouth to speak. But what to say?

He grasped her forearm. The creases of his fingers were black, the nails long and yellow, his middle finger stained with nicotine. "May you manifest our unity at the end of the matrix." He looked down at the head again and squeezed her arm. "Know that you are loved."

He placed his hands in prayer position with his thumbs touching his forehead and bowed slightly. Trish could feel her eyes wide, her head shoved back on her neck to get as much distance as possible from the man, who indeed smelled of unity. He didn't look at her again but pushed away on his roller blades. His guitar was missing a string.

As the man faded into the crowd, Trish did not know she was loved but desired that feeling strongly. She texted Luca.

> Boo, I'm struggling
> with this thing.

She wanted him to come to her, wished they could be together for this thing. Like Preeta's exercise. Maybe the head would finally be enough to compel him to come to her. If only he would say he loved her.

> I know. You need to
> figure it out. Sorry.

He would not even say he loved her. Trish's eyes grew wide as she looked up from the phone and a chill of realization settled over her. She had always been sympathetic to Luca's circumstances. But it had been misplaced.

Now, more than anything, Trish wanted her mother—the sense of equanimity that came with her mother's pride. Her mother would know how to put things right. Her mother would understand how this thing was interfering with the life she wanted to live. She texted Jess.

> I'm thinking about going
> to see my mum.

Oh? For Christmas?

> No. Now.

What? How? Don't
you have to teach?

> I've taken a leave.

What?! What happened?

Is this why you were
scared yesterday?
Is it about Luca? I
was worried he would
cause problems.

> You didn't like him because
> he's conservative, not cuz of
> how it would look at work.

I DIDN'T LIKE him
because he's right wing.
I was worried because of
how it would look at work.

The bubbles stopped and the phone lit up in Trish's hand.

"What is going on?" The rhythm of Jess's footsteps bumped into her words.

"I'm overwhelmed. The world's really weird."

"You're stressed out about work. It doesn't help that buddy ditched you."

"It's not him. I just… what if I've misunderstood what the world's all about? What if the higher dimensions…" Trish looked around to be sure no one was listening. Her upper body was suddenly very heavy. She bent at the waist and put her head on the seawall.

"Why don't you come here? Come here instead of going to see your mother."

How pathetic Trish was. Thoughtlessly machinating her way into this poor woman's sympathies and life. Jess was also working toward tenure, maintaining her research and teaching. But she was managing to keep up her responsibilities, and now she had to offer succour to some wretched friend.

"No, no. I'm fine. You're so busy. Let's plan. We should plan a visit."

"Or you could come now."

"I'm gonna get a lot of work done. It's gonna be good. Just add to the tenure application."

"Oh please. If your application got any stronger, you'd go straight from assistant to full professor. Fuck their mediocre associate bullshit."

An ember of heat pierced her belly from the fanny pack and the head started to cry. A piteous little whine.

"Trish, it's just stressful. You don't need to question everything."

She nodded into the phone and hung up. She needed to call her mother.

CHAPTER SEVEN

Deidre worked from home painting landscapes for hotels. She had stumbled upon the skill and the market during an evening class, which she had signed up for because she had "always wanted to be an artist," though Trish had never heard her express a desire to paint or heard her admire landscapes especially. But Deidre had impressed a classmate who purchased art for a chain of hotels. The woman was in the class "to understand my artists," as if she owned a gallery and made any difference to the art world and was not hotel-chain middle management. By the end of the six-week course, Trish's mother had a commission from the hotel chain to produce six paintings of the prairies and foothills around Brookbridge, which they would then reproduce for their southern locations. The first commission led to a second and a third and then Trish lost track of all the work her mother had and all the places her art was "shown."

Early in her painting career, at the end of Trish's final year of high school, a brand-new boutique hotel commissioned her to paint several landscapes for their rooms, as well as two big paintings for the lobby. The hotel hosted a grand opening party, which Deidre referred to as "my opening." Trish was bringing a friend to the opening and was in her room getting ready when the friend texted that she was downstairs waiting. When she opened the door of her room, she could hear a voice in the house that was unfamiliar—lisping and lilting. She stood listening in the hall, breathing quietly so she could hear.

"Is Daddy proud of his girl?"

Trish tiptoed to her parents' room and saw her mother in just a bra and panties on her father's lap at the edge of the bed, straightening Tony's tie.

"Maybe I deserve a reward?" Deidre tilted her head at a coquettish angle.

"Well." Tony squeezed Deidre's thigh tightly. "We'll see about that."

Trish moved quietly to the top of the stairs and then thumped loudly down to retrieve her friend.

At the event, Trish avoided her father and when Deidre was asked to say a few words, Trish stared at the tabletop as her mother spoke coherently about her work and the role of small business in a vibrant local economy. Throughout the evening, when Deidre introduced Trish, she would say it was a relief that Trish was going to MIT in the fall so she could finally give her painting the attention it deserved.

And indeed, the fall that Trish started university, her mother left her administration job at the local community health clinic to paint full-time. A local "art-dealer" began to commission her for paintings, which would then appear on cards and mugs and magnets at local tourist stops. When Trish came home from university, Deidre would insist they go into these stores where she would offer to sign the cards and prints on sale.

One time, she went to the counter and asked, "Do you have anything by Deidre Russo?"

The poor kid behind the counter said, "I don't know who that is," as he turned to check his computer for inventory.

Deidre tapped her finger on the counter, "You should."

Trish drifted away to look at knick-knacks and printed dish towels.

"I'm glad I could do that for them," Deidre whispered on the way back out the door.

As Trish made her way through graduate school and university became her career, she and her mother began to talk about "work." Deidre loved that they both had work that was "their passion." Trish did not love having her work in math equated with bad hotel paintings, but it was a relief that her mother saw her as an equal and she came to rely upon her mother's expressions of support as a gauge for her work and career path. When Trish began to attend international conferences, Deidre saw the opportunity to "expand into other markets" and began travelling with Trish to network and show her work. In the evenings, Deidre would regale tables full of mathematicians with a who's who of hotel art commissioning. When a conference organizer told Deidre that Trish had won the conference prize for best paper, Deidre said, "Oh I wish I'd known earlier! I met a buyer today who was very interested in academia."

Now the ringing phone sent hope through Trish's chest.

"Well, this is a pleasant surprise."

"I have a bigger surprise. I'm coming to see you."

"Oh great. We were just talking about Christmas."

"No. I've got some free time now, and I thought I'd come."

"Now? That's unusual, isn't it? Is there a break at the university? Such a cushy job, teaching."

Trish couldn't control her breathing. She stopped walking. "I just need a bit of a break. These grant applications. I'm overwhelmed."

"Weren't you planning to come at Christmas?"

"I hadn't thought about Christmas yet."

"Okay, well, I think Christmas is a good idea. Come at Christmas. That will be lovely."

Why on earth were they talking about Christmas? Trish shook her head. "Okay, yes. I can come at Christmas. But I was also thinking I could come now. I have a few days."

"Well, no, no. That's not necessary. Not if you're coming at Christmas. Save your money."

"I was thinking it would be nice though."

"It's just… it's not great timing, Trish. I have… I'm painting and I have meetings. But at Christmas people will expect me to have family to deal with."

How was Deidre not picking up on Trish's need? The urgency? She was going to have to steel herself. "Something's going on and I feel like I need you. I need my mum."

"You're a perfectly capable young woman. I'm sure there's nothing I can contribute."

Trish held on in silence.

Deidre sighed. "Alright, alright. Come if you want. I'll have to work while you're here though."

"I want to work too."

After she booked her flight, she texted her mother the arrival time, and her mother replied that she would need to rent a car and meet her at the gallery.

Cam had texted while Trish booked her flight.

Where are you? People
are saying you've
gone on leave??

The sun was setting. Trish looked down at the little head nestled inside its fanny pack. She wanted to get it home.

Cam started as assistant professor in the math department when he was twenty-five. Many of the department's grad students were older. After a few months, Trish noticed that he was spending a lot of time in her office sitting in the chair beside her desk, cracking jokes, reeling off bizarre statistics, and asking if she wanted to get coffee or lunch. When Trish realized he was not just popping by as a collegial pleasantry, she felt herself move a notch closer to "reasonable human" status. Reasonable humans have friends; reasonable humans have friends with benefits. Cam and Luca could never know about each other. But people see what they want to see, so that would be easily managed.

But as it unfolded, her friendship with Cam made apparent how far she had to go before she was, in fact, a reasonable human. On days when they made plans, Trish would avoid eating all day to save the calories for eating out or having a beer that night. But she could not just fast like a normal person. If she didn't eat, by late afternoon her stomach would start to bloat painfully, at which point not even food could help. In fact, food on top of the bloat was incredibly painful.

Once, Cam cancelled after the bloating started and so Trish went home and lay on her bed. She could feel the gas move slowly through her gut until she let out several enormous farts. When she got back up after about an hour, she was fine and ate ramen noodles for dinner in front of the television. So now she knew. Farting helped with the bloating. But Cam rarely cancelled. And sitting in her office in anticipation of the evening out, Trish could not force herself to fart. She spent evenings with Cam with a gut that looked like it was going to burst, which she then had to suck in when they got naked. The significant pain was a measure of the absurdity of the woman's life.

Now, Cam's text was a lifeline to the outside world.

> Yeah. Tang put me on leave.
> But hey. I'm at the beach.

What are you
talking about?

Why?

> Apparently I've upset my grad
> students. Scared them. If I go
> away, so does the problem.

They can't put you on
leave just because your
grad students don't
want to have to think.

> Yeah it's not just that. It was
> me. But I'm still shocked
> at their lack of loyalty.

They can't even be loyal to
their own research. I don't
see why you're surprised.

> I'm especially shocked
> at Brandon.

Really? The kid's
name is Brandon.

> Do you want to hang out?

That's what I was thinking.

> Can you come to my place?

> I'm going to see my mother
> and I have an early flight.

Sure. I'm still at school.
I'll leave in half an hour.

The plan gave her confidence and she wanted to text Luca—show him she was okay without him. But it would only have the opposite effect.

On the walk home, Trish was not sure that she wanted Cam to come over. The matter of the head felt so pressing. Cam was not keen to offer empathy, if he felt it at all. But hanging out with a friend the night before you go away is something a normal person would do. Someone who didn't have a disembodied head in their kitchen drawer. Besides, people hung out with friends when they were in distress too. Cam's company should bring relief. Maybe tonight. At least she had eaten throughout the day, so she wasn't bloated.

As she turned away from the beach and up the street to her apartment, Trish texted Jess.

> I booked my flight.
> Tomorrow morning.

You could come here
instead. We could
get doughnuts from
this new place that
opened downtown.

> I'm not fit for public
> consumption.

You packing?

Cam's coming over.

But you can't come
here for doughnuts.

She watched Cam's back as he untied his shoes.

"I waited. I wasn't going to order Chinese without you."

He raised his eyebrows. "That's racist."

"C'mon. Just the other day you told me how you're such a pro at ordering Chinese that the wait staff talks to you in Mandarin."

"They do. One time me and Jay…"

"Wait. I'm so hungry. Can we just order please?"

She waved her phone in front of his face, the order form for the restaurant open.

"Fiiiine." He took her phone, scrolled and clicked and threw himself onto the couch. "I'll give you a single choice."

"General Tao?"

"White people are embarrassing."

"You didn't have to ask! And! You're half Irish! They don't come much whiter."

"Even in County Cork, General Tao is not Chinese food. It's fine." He handed her back the phone. "Half an hour."

A cramp started on the left side of her stomach, just up from her hip. She wanted to talk about the head. The desire for sympathy and understanding was a pressure in her head that she could not think around. There was nothing else to talk about. Cam would not want to hear it. How distressing it was. And he could not give her the sympathy she wanted either.

Still, the pressure for the sympathy was there. The urge to say something about it was a bubble at the back of her mouth.

"Things are really weird for me right now."

"Yeah. What's going on? Do you still have that thing you brought to the meeting yesterday?" Cam looked around the living room for evidence of the head.

"Yeah. I wish it would just disappear the same way it appeared. I can't think. I can't work."

"Maybe you have ADHD?"

"Can you get a PhD with ADHD?"

"Oh, yeah. People learn to manage it but then their coping mechanisms stop working or just aren't sufficient anymore. Women are frequently not diagnosed until later in life because the demands of childrearing prevent them from focusing on their careers until much later."

"Is thirty older?"

"No. I think it's more like fifty. But you look good for your age." Cam smiled to signal that he was joking.

Trish could not imagine having her career delayed for almost as long as she'd been alive. "I just feel like the world's not what I thought it was, you know?"

"How's that grant proposal coming?"

"Not that. Something more fundamental, you know?"

"Listen, you're not driving a pickup truck with a gun rack and a Confederate flag. You're doing okay."

"That's a pretty low bar."

"Then reality *is* different than what you thought."

"Let's choose a movie."

When the food arrived, Trish took it into the kitchen to put it on plates and glanced at the drawer where the head remained quiet. Was it asleep? Could she open the drawer and check on it without Cam seeing and deriding her for it?

The cramp in her stomach spread out from her left hip and sat across her entire pelvis. Eating now would probably make it worse. But she could hardly not eat now that they'd ordered.

As they watched the movie, Trish chewed and swallowed slowly and imagined how she was going to introduce the topic of the head to her mother. If only she didn't have to show her father. Over and over, in her mind's eye, he sneered at the head. At her.

When she got up to clear the dishes, a sharp pain stabbed into Trish's chest. In the kitchen the head squeaked in its drawer. The urge to check on it was an imperative. She needed to be alone. Back in the living room, she sat on Cam's lap, facing him, her arms over his shoulders.

"I can't see."

"Mm." She kissed him.

"You don't care."

"No." She pulled his shirt up over his head.

"Well, this is going quickly."

"I have an early flight."

"Right. I'm cold. Come lie on top of me."

Cam lay down and Trish tossed aside her own shirt and bra, grabbed the blanket from the end of the couch and lay down beside him. She undid his jeans and slid a hand into his pants. "Take these off." She yanked at a belt loop.

As she took off her own pants, Trish pulled in her stomach so that the bloat from the cramps and the food didn't show, then she straddled him, keeping her shoulders back to show off her breasts. She stroked his penis until it was hard. But as she reached down to put it inside her, a vision of the head rose in her mind's eye and brought heat and nausea. Maybe without the stomach cramps, she could have persevered, but it was too much.

She let out a long "uuuuhn," and lowered her head to Cam's chest, keeping her butt in the air. The nausea morphed into an angry dagger in her diaphragm.

"You okay?" Cam looked at her sideways.

Which would be more mortifying? *I can't have sex until I've had about an hour alone to fart,* or *I can't have sex because of the disembodied head in my tea towel drawer?*

"I don't know what's wrong. I don't feel great."

Trish sat back on her heels and Cam's knees. He sat up and tried to put his arms around her but she dropped past him and put her head into the space on the couch he just vacated, pulling her legs off him. He put his shirt on and handed Trish hers, which she spread across her breasts.

"Thanks. Sorry."

Cam covered her with the blanket, turned off the TV and sat looking at Trish. The pain in her diaphragm spread up into her sternum. Maybe she was having a heart attack.

"I don't know what to say," she said by way of apology.

"Did you know that a language goes extinct every two weeks?"

Trish hated it when he said something interesting. She did not want to encourage him. "How can that be? How many languages are there?"

"Almost seven thousand, currently."

"Math is more powerful anyway."

"Certainly. Though"—Cam tilted his head back and forth in consideration—"from enrollment rates over the past forty years, you could argue that math is in danger of extinction."

"How do they know?"

"About the languages?" Cam shrugged. "The silence, I guess."

After Cam left, Trish put on pajamas, rubbing her swollen belly and aching chest. She went to the kitchen and opened the tea towel drawer. Moist minty heat wafted up. The head was asleep on its side, the damp facecloth under its cheek.

"Tsk."

She lifted the head away from the damp. It was soft and made her think of warm baths and flannel. She cradled the head in her palm, took a fresh towel for it to suck on, and carried the thing to bed.

CHAPTER EIGHT

Scene of the crime echoed through Trish's mind again as she stepped into the shower before her flight the next morning. Hyperbolic. Besides, the shower wasn't even really the scene of the crime. It was just the place where she had first heard the head—first been made aware of its existence. The scene of the crime was really her bedroom. The dresser in her bedroom.

A jet of water hit her ribs and another recurring dream from her childhood sprang across her skin. This one started a few years after she stopped having the troll dream but while the troll dream still haunted her. In this dream, a witch held her tightly and tickled her ribcage with long fingernails. Trish could feel it now—this otherworldly terror holding her so tightly and touching her so intimately. During the year or so when she had the dream, the sensation would foist itself upon her throughout the day. Years after the dream stopped, she still felt the tickle. She would call it up in her early-morning first-year physics class. Now Trish remembered that when she invoked it, she would also imagine her father's oily hair, and let a wave of revulsion pass through her body. Astonishing to think that the feelings had gone and she could not even remember when they left.

Normally, Trish could sleepwalk through the trip from Cascadia to Brookbridge, where her parents lived. But she had never made the trip with a disembodied head. She booked the flight through Fletcher Field, Cascadia's smaller airport and hoped that if the head stayed quiet, things would be fine. But what if it started to cry? Was she going to claim it was a support animal? She imagined the security guards pulling her into a room, the head shrieking on a grey metal desk, police in baggy yellow biohazard suits, the flappy hats with welder goggles to see through. She could tell them it was some new technology they were inventing at Cascadia. That would impress them. She could show them her staff card. They didn't need to know she taught math.

In its purse, the head was not heavy or awkward, but its weight and heat, and the rhythmic bounce against her belly as she walked, set up a hive-like buzz just under her skin. She passed through the airport's sliding glass doors and stopped, unsure how to proceed.

"Excuse me." A woman's suitcase knocked against Trish's. "You're right in the doorway."

Her boarding pass was already on her phone. She wasn't checking any luggage. Security, then. Straight to security. She inhaled deeply.

In the back-and-forth line for security, the head began to cry. Of course. The woman ahead of her craned her neck and looked around. When she looked back at Trish, she did a double take but then smiled politely. As the line lurched forward, the head's cries grew louder. Now more people were looking around for the crying baby. Trish's face burned. Where the line tacked back towards her, a couple began to whisper.

The woman in front of Trish turned around again. "Is your phone ringing?"

Like an idiot, Trish looked down at her purse. Between her breasts, her shirt was dotted with sweat. "I keep it on silent."

The woman's brow wrinkled and she followed Trish's gaze to the purse. She shook her head as she stared at the purse. "I keep thinking I hear a weird alarm or something."

Trish's shirt felt glued to her armpits. Maybe she could get a new one in the gift shop once she was through security. That could be fun. Maybe she could find something nice.

At the conveyor belt she put her computer and pack in the bins. Normally, in a stand for decency, Trish resisted the appalling practice of removing your shoes and waited until instructed to do so. This time though she bent to untie her shoes and then stood to be waved through the screening gate.

"Ma'am, your purse," an agent called from the other side, his thumbs hooked in his belt.

"Oh gosh. Can't it come through with me?"

It was not the dumbest question he would hear today, and he couldn't know she wasn't the dumbest person he would see all day. "No ma'am. Put it in the bin."

If the head went through the scanner in a bin, the heat sensors would pick it up. Trish imagined dashing through the arch with the purse still over her shoulder. The scanner would not beep and that should satisfy them. She would be a hero for proving all this nonsense at security was unnecessary. People would thank her.

Everything seemed very far away. There was a static in the air, and the sounds of the airport were dulled and delayed, as if they were underwater. There was nothing else to do. Trish put the purse down gently in a bin. The agent behind the arch was already waving her through the people scanner and now Trish hurried so as not to irritate him further. Once across the threshold, she put her shoes on but did not take the time to lace them. She stood and watched the image on the scanner's screen. On the monitor, the head appeared as an orange circle with deep red and bright yellow highlights. The woman at the monitor toggled the image a few times.

"That's mine," Trish called. "It's nothing, don't worry about it."

The agent glanced back at Trish while a male security guard bent over her shoulder and peered into the screen. He said something to the woman. Trish should not have spoken. The woman advanced the belt through the scanner so the bin with the purse popped out the car-wash flaps. The man pulled on new plastic surgical gloves, seized the edge of the bin, and pointed at Trish with his chin. The purse slid around at the bottom of the bin and the head cried. Trish met the man at the end of the belt.

"I'm going to need to inspect your bag, ma'am. Do I have your permission?"

Trish stared at the purse, sweat trickled down her back.

"Ma'am."

"It's nothing. It's just like… like…"

Trish rubbed her index fingers against her thumbs to indicate texture. Even Trish did not understand the relevance of the gesture. Futile.

People passed behind Trish, craning their necks to watch.

"Ma'am, I am going to look inside your purse."

Trish nodded.

Leaving the purse in the bin, the man opened the top flap and lifted the edge as if he was to tea with the Queen. He bent sideways and peered from arm's length into the dark opening from various angles and heights, his face contorting before each move. Finally he shook his head, stood to his full height and, eyes heavenward, reached into the purse. Holding it like an apple, the guard presented Trish with the head, which blinked quietly in his hand. A small consolation.

"Ma'am, what is this?"

"It's not dangerous."

The woman behind her said, "It's some kind of toy. They have these lifelike pets for the elderly now. This one's not nice at all."

"She's right," Trish almost shouted. "It's a toy. Like one of those fake cats. It's more like a Tamagotchi. Remember those? You have to care for it and…"

The agent squinted.

"That ain't no Tamagotchi."

"No, no. It's new. It's brand-new technology. I work at Cascadia. We're developing these robots. Companions. They're supposed to help people feel less lonely, less isolated."

He held the head up to look at its underside and shook his head, then walked back to the woman at the scanner. He showed her the head and pointed back to Trish who tried to smile. The woman shook her head at something the guard said.

"The scanner didn't pick up that it was electronic."

Trish's hollow chest and throat. "It's, um, it's just a prototype."

The guard narrowed his eyes and sniffed scornfully. Like he could make a better prototype. He walked with the head to a small station behind him and ran a piece of gauze over its face and back. He put the gauze into a small machine and closed the lid. A few seconds later, the machine beeped, and a green light flashed. The guard threw the gauze into a garbage bin beside the stand and came back with the head.

"Alright," he handed Trish the head. "It's no danger."

"Thank you."

Trish took the head from him and wiped its cheeks.

"But you should know. That thing's no comfort either."

Trish tried to smile and held the head against her breast, relieved to have it back in her hands. She carried it cupped to her chest as she pulled her carry-on out of security into the waiting area and maneuvered the purchase of a bottle of water with one hand. The water at the back of her throat brought her back to herself. She was safe. She had the head, and they were both safe.

Not since she was seven years old had she been so desperate for a window seat. With her back turned to her neighbour, Trish cradled the head in her hands and stroked its soft face as she stared out at the landscape below.

At the Brookbridge airport, Trish rented a car and drove straight to the art gallery. Her mother was in the gift shop, chatting to the store manager. "There she is!"

She waved both hands above her head and then put her arms around Trish as she came into the store. "Trish is a math professor," Deidre told the store manager as she released Trish. "She gets her ability with numbers from her father."

This claim always made Trish want to explain the difference between mathematics and accountancy. "Only an artist would think so." Trish tried to sound like she was joking and not just being petty. Maybe the "artist" would be enough cushion. But Deidre froze and the store manager's eyes grew wide.

"Well, speaking of math, I should get back to my inventory."

Out in the lobby, Deidre was still unwilling to give Trish her attention. "So," she clasped her hands in front of her, "What are you interested in seeing? We could start with the permanent exhibit? There's a terrific quilting exhibit in the smaller gallery upstairs. Really compelling works."

"That sounds nice. Can we do that after? Can we sit and have coffee first?"

Inside the gallery's cafe, Deidre turned off the presentation of herself as tour guide to the gallery. "It's good you're here, actually. It turns out I can use your help to move some canvases this weekend."

"Okay, we can do that. There's just something I need to talk to you about first. I need your help." Trish's heart was racing. Her thin, shallow breath was drying out the back of her throat. Deidre raised an expectant eyebrow.

"Yeah, God. I don't really know how to start." Trish opened the flap of the head's purse.

"Oh, you still use that. I bought you that, didn't I?"

"You did. I use it all the time." For the past forty-eight hours, that had been true.

Trish pulled the sleeping head out of the purse and held it in her open palm above the table. Deidre gasped, put her hand to her mouth and jumped back in her chair.

"I'm sorry. I didn't mean to scare you. I know—it's scary. Sorry. I shouldn't have…"

What an idiot. Of course the thing was going to upset Deidre. It was upsetting. Trish drew it back down and held it close so that her mother couldn't see it. "This is what I need help with. I don't know what to do. It just came to me. It just appeared on my dresser a couple of days ago."

"What do you mean, 'it appeared'?"

"I was in the shower. It was my birthday. I got up and it wasn't there and then in the shower I kept hearing these weird noises and when I got out, it was lying on my dresser, crying."

"Crying?"

"I've learned how to keep it a bit quieter now."

"It's some kind of toy?" At the airport it had been a relief when the woman suggested the idea of a toy. Now it was perplexing and exhausting to have to explain the thing.

"No. Mum. It's not a toy. It just showed up. I'm scared. I'm quite scared. I don't know why it came to me and I don't know what to do with it. I'm sure I'm supposed to do something. But I don't know what and I'm so scared of what will happen if I don't do the right thing! I mean, it's bad enough that I've had this thing foisted upon me. What if I get it wrong?"

"Are you okay? Were you hurt?"

"Hurt? No, I wasn't hurt. It was just there. I have no idea where it came from. All I know is that it's distressing, and it needs me. It needs me."

They were the only customers in the restaurant, but they whispered so as not to attract the attention of the wait staff.

"Well, someone must have put it there."

"No, no. There was no sign that anyone had broken in. The doors were locked. The windows were locked. No one came in. It doesn't make sense that someone left it."

"Did you call the police?"

"I didn't think I should. I thought they would think I was crazy. I kind of presumed it was my fault. That, like, I was crazy enough to cause this. Anyway, I had to go to work. I didn't have time to take it to the police."

"They would have come to you."

"I had a faculty meeting."

"Are you not teaching this semester?"

Trish waved the question away. "Do you think I'm crazy? Do you think it's my fault?" A layer of frost spread from her scalp to the skin of her neck and shoulders.

"I don't know what to think. It's so unbelievable. 'Crazy' and 'fault' though—those are very loaded."

"You know what I mean." Trish rolled her hand to hurry her mother along.

"I am concerned. I am concerned for you. I wouldn't say I'm concerned about you because I think you're safe from outside interference. But I am concerned *for* you."

"I really need you to say I'm not crazy."

"You're not crazy. You're obviously not yourself. I think we need to address the cause of that."

The head let out a tremendous shriek. Trish and Deidre both jumped. Deidre glanced at the wait staff who had also jumped at the sound and were now trying not to stare at the two women with a disembodied head between them.

"You see!" Trish's eyes were wide, pleading. "What am I supposed to do?! I feel like I'm losing my mind. I don't know what I'm supposed to do!"

She started to cry and shushed down into her lap. At least that hid her face from her mother. A tear fell into one of the head's eyes. It squeezed them shut and roared.

"Sh. Sh. Sh." Trish bounced the head under the table, urging the cloth on it. Deidre's eyes were wide. "Sorry. It likes to suck on these facecloths. I don't know why it cries." Trish squeezed her eyes tight and shook her head hard to clear it. "I really don't know why it cries."

Deidre gave a tight smile to the wait staff.

"I'm sorry. I'll try to stop."

"If you could. This is effectively my place of work."

Trish nodded and took a deep breath through her nose.

"Now, why don't we put the thing away and have a nice, pleasant lunch?"

"Mum, I can't just put it away. I need to take care of it. Attend to it. I can't just leave it unattended!"

Deidre sat up straight, pursed her lips in a tight smile and waved the waitress over. "A glass of white, please. Whatever's open."

"I'm sorry. I'm just really scared. I know you're super busy and so I'm sorry to come to you like this. I just really don't know what to do and I don't want to bother anyone. I know it's such a freaky thing. It's weird and hard to look at. Who even wants to look at it, let alone help me with it!"

"Okay, I've heard enough for now." Deidre's hand darted across the table and snatched the head. Trish's fingers fell in like a mouth with no teeth.

"What are you doing?!" Trish threw herself across the table but in a single swift motion, Deidre had stuffed the head into her own purse and hung it on the back of her chair.

"Trish, you need to forget this thing." Deidre folded her hands on the table, her back straight and long. "Ah! You're an angel," she sang to the waitress and the wine as it was placed in front of her. "You cannot believe the day we're having here."

The waitress raised her eyebrows and one corner of her mouth. They had not improved her day either.

"Trish, you need to forget this thing," Deidre repeated. "I don't know what you've done, or how you've acquired this thing."

"I didn't *do* anything! Can I have it back, please? It needs me."

"There's obviously something you're not telling me. If you were innocent in this, then you would be willing to call the police."

"I just don't see what the police can do!"

"Well, it's too late now anyway. The fact that you waited so long would just point to your guilt, really."

"What would the police even investigate?"

"If you're innocent, then someone obviously broke into your apartment."

"I really didn't see any signs of a break in."

"That's the thing, Trish. You don't know everything. The police could have helped you figure that out. Clear you."

"Look," Trish dropped her head and whispered, "I don't know how I know, okay. I just know that it just showed up." How to explain that one could make effective assumptions from visual proofs?

"How am I supposed to believe that?" Deidre emptied her wine and waved for another.

"Lots of things are true that we can't experience with our senses. They're very limited, our senses. I work with proofs all the time of things that are beyond our sensory possibilities."

Deidre took the wine from the waitress before she could even set it on the table. "Maybe you were not in your right mind. Maybe you had a psychotic break or something."

Inside Deidre's purse, the head screeched. Trish couldn't blame it. All the wait staff jumped and stared before clustering together in front of the bar, their backs to Trish and Deidre.

"Can I have the head please?"

"Trish, how do you benefit from insisting on this thing? You don't. No one's going to believe your crazy story. No one's going to take you seriously."

Trish's head filled with a roar like the ocean on a stormy day.

"Trish!" Deidre called to her across the sound. "It's not what you think it is."

"Then why do I feel like it needs me?"

Deidre threw her hands up in disgust. "I don't typically believe in these things but maybe you've become involved in some satanic ritual or something?"

"What? No. What do you mean *become involved in*? I would know if I was involved in a cult!"

"I said I don't believe in them. But maybe that's what's happening here."

"What? If you don't believe in them…?"

"I'm just trying to be open to possibilities."

As a scholar, Trish commended her mother's willingness to take in new evidence. "I've been remembering all these dreams I had as a kid. These recurring nightmares. And I remember that I was scared a lot of the time when I was a kid."

"Don't be ridiculous. You were not. You had everything you could want and more. In fact, you never learned to think of anyone but yourself. You have never understood how to be part of a family. You still think you're the centre of the universe. That the world would manifest this disgusting thing so you could care for it."

"I don't *want* it. I didn't ask for it."

"You think that. But you're not saying no to it either. You can't handle even a modicum of responsibility—anyone asking anything of you except that you be left to your other dimensions that no one else understands." Deidre rolled her eyes at "other dimensions."

"Higher. Higher dimensions. People understand," Trish tried. "Other mathematicians." A streak of sun came through the window and lit the water glass on the table. Trish squinted out through the window.

"You chose math so that you didn't have to participate in the real world and look at what happens as soon as you're under any pressure at work. As soon as you're no longer just the golden child, you end up dragging some disgusting thing around, telling some story about how it needs you."

The ray of light faded from the tabletop as one of the wait staff lowered the electronic blinds. Once the shades were drawn, Deidre waved for the bill.

Outside the cafe, Trish suggested they check out the gallery. "The quilts sounded nice."

Deidre held her purse open at Trish's diaphragm so she could take the head. "I just need to go home. Where did you park? I took the train down."

In the car, Trish put the purse in the back seat so that her mother could sit in the passenger seat. "I hope it will be alright back there."

Deidre raised her eyebrows as she buckled up. "Trish, stop already. Look at what you're doing to yourself. You're ruining your life with this thing."

"What am I supposed to do?!"

"I mean you could start by not caring. The least you could do is ignore the damn thing."

The idea was not entirely unappealing. And was this not why she had wanted her mother—for down-to-earth guidance back to her normal life? If she ignored the head, she could go back to Cascadia and just pick up her grant application and the hiring committee. She could put her teaching evaluations back together over time. Take on some service work. If she could be free of the head again, then she would finally be a reasonable human being. The question was how not to feel its need and its heat.

Trish turned her attention to the view through the windshield and put the keys in the ignition. As she drove, she ignored the cries of the head until, finally, they stopped.

"You're right." She kept her eyes on the road. "It feels better to forget it." She took a deep breath in the silence of the car. "I'm sorry," Trish whispered.

Deidre reached over and squeezed Trish's hand on the steering wheel.

CHAPTER NINE

Trish attended her high school graduation dinner with a group of girlfriends. She genuinely liked her friends' families, but was also aware that she did not belong with them. Even as she enjoyed their company, she knew they didn't, wouldn't, couldn't want her. Not honestly. Or, if honestly, then not intimately.

It also put her off balance that her father was there. He was so little a presence in her life. How was it sensible that he should be at this event to mark a significant milestone? Trish ignored him as diligently as possible. His slick hair and shiny suit made her queasy.

Early in the evening, before dinner was served, while the parents were drinking cocktails and different friends and families were clustering around the table to chat, another father congratulated Tony on Trish's achievements.

Tony laughed too loudly, "It's amazing how far the occasional hand job will take a girl these days."

The other parents around the table tittered in response and Trish's friends stared at their hands.

Deidre smacked him playfully and laughed, "Oh Tony!" She waved away the tension at the table, "What a joker!"

Tony shrugged and drained his whiskey.

Panic rang painfully through Trish's head, setting her face on fire. She had never told anyone about that afternoon with Mr. Rose when she touched his hand, when she came on to him. Trish knew it was true that the only thing her parents knew was that she did extra work with the math teacher. But her father's statement now fractured that truth and another truth was created, which peeled away into a second truth with the same dimensions but different shadows, where it was the case that they knew she had embarrassed herself by making a pass at Mr. Rose. This first set of truths split again into a second set of truth and shadow-truth. It was true that nothing untoward had happened with Mr. Rose; but now a reality also existed wherein Trish had used sex with him to succeed in high school and get into university. The reality of the first truths did not extend past Trish's skin, where they jostled with her guilt over the second shadowy truths which, she was sure, were now everyone else's shared reality.

Later that night, Trish came in from her grad after-party, tiptoeing through the kitchen so as not to wake her parents. As she came into the darkened living room, she saw her mother sitting facing her father on his lap, her eyes lowered coquettishly.

"Ooh, teacher, you know such big numbers." She drew out the word 'big,' her pitch soft. "Teach me a *wesson*."

Eyes wide, Trish turned on her toes and crept back through the kitchen to the door, which she opened quietly and then slammed loudly. She made a show of grunting while she pulled off her shoes before she banged open a cupboard for a glass and threw on the overhead light, running the water full blast into the sink. When she finally walked through the living room, her parents were gone.

Trish showed the head to her father when he came home from work. He always left his briefcase in the hall with his shoes and went directly to his chair in the living room, where Deidre brought him a drink.

As he took off his shoes, Deidre said, "Trish has come into possession of something fairly strange and she wants us to help her."

"Unless it's a stash of gold bullion, I don't see what I can offer."

Deidre laughed genuinely, "Wouldn't that be nice."

As he came into the living room. Trish held out the head for him to see before he had a chance to bring her in for his standard kiss on the lips.

"What the hell is that thing?" He picked it up with his thumb and index finger, his lips curled. Trish fought panic as he brought it up to eye level and inspected it like you might a sea cucumber.

"I just found it on my dresser a few days ago—on my birthday. I don't know. I don't know what it is. I need help. I can't go back to work with it."

Tony narrowed his eyes at her. She was sick of hearing herself tell the story. She wasn't going to tell it again.

"Let me get you a drink," Deidre offered.

"Yes. Please. Jesus." He turned back to Trish. "You took this to work?" But he didn't want an answer. Just went back to inspecting the thing. "It has to be some kind of joke. A prank."

He held the head up to the light and ran his fingers over the skin tags along its bottom. The head closed its eyes and made small wet noises under his fingers. Trish felt vaguely betrayed.

Tony handed the head back to Trish with an exaggerated shiver. She smoothed the delicate hairs on its head. It sighed and a small burble of reassurance welled up in her chest.

"How the hell am I supposed to know what to do with that thing?" He sank into his chair. "Why would you hang on to such a thing? It's obvious someone hates you."

Deidre came around and handed him the drink. Then she sat on the arm of the chair, her arm over his shoulder. "Mm," she wobbled her head back and forth in consideration. "Yes. That seems reasonable, doesn't it?"

"It's some kind of payback. Retribution." He pointed at Trish with his drink. "The horse's head!"

"What have you done, Trish?" Deidre asked.

"No. Nothing. I haven't done anything to deserve this."

"Well, no one's saying you deserve *this*. But someone obviously thinks you deserve *something*."

Trish's mind raced over the possibilities again. There was no one specific person. Maybe her father was right? Maybe this was just how deeply the universe hated her? Her unsuitability for her work. The world. Her uselessness in all aspects of the world. Her pathetic existence. Retribution for her pathetic existence.

"I don't think there was anyone involved. I don't think it came from a person."

Deidre sat silently on the arm of Tony's chair. Tony shook his head and tossed back the rest of his drink. Without speaking, he handed it across his chest to Deidre for a refill. "That's one weird kid you've got there, Deeds."

Deidre kissed the top of his head as she handed him a fresh drink and then sat at the other end of the couch from Trish.

Tony took a sip from his drink. "Sorry—maybe I missed something. Why have you not just chucked it?"

Suddenly Trish was crying. "Daddy, I don't know! It needs me or something. It's alive. And it's come into my care. I need to take care of it!" Trish put her face in her hands and sobbed. In her lap, the head jostled back and forth slightly as if in a boat on a lake. "I'm so scared." It was barely a whisper.

Tony came over to Trish and put his arm around her. She

let him pull her closer so the full length of her arm lay along his body.

He had comforted her one other time. She was home from her first semester of university and none of the clothes she'd left behind fit anymore. Sitting on her childhood bed she cried, "Do you still love me?"

He pulled her into him, "Don't be ridiculous. Of course I still love you." That time she felt genuine relief when he laughed at her.

"Let's get you a glass of water."

Tony looked to Deidre, who stood to get the water. While she was away, Tony smoothed Trish's hair. She stopped crying. Deidre handed Trish the water and the cool was refreshing on her throat. She sat back and her breath stuttered in a sigh.

"I just feel like it needs my care. Like I'm responsible for it. But at the same time, I'm just so ashamed."

"That's understandable."

"You think I should be ashamed?"

"I think there's nothing to be ashamed of if you were just getting on with your life. But you're dragging this thing around. Insisting on it."

"I feel like it needs my care. Like it's mine somehow. Like it's the least I could do." Trish addressed her father, and then wondered out loud, "Is it how I redeem myself?"

"Redeem yourself? Trish, you're actively ruining everything by dragging this head around. It's a talisman of horror and you're walking around subjecting people to it. You come here expecting our sympathy…" Her father stood and went back to his chair. "I don't know what you did to deserve this thing. But it's disgusting and distressing. Nobody wants to see it. The way to 'redeem yourself' is to stop showing it to people!"

Trish looked over at her mother who raised her eyebrow in an *I-told-you-so* expression. Trish was aware that she was not thinking. Aware of herself as an existence outside of, beyond, thought. In that space, she was hollow, simply empty.

"Ha!" Tony smirked as he chewed ice from his drink. "You know what you should do with that thing? Hang it on a leather thong around your neck!"

Deidre's laughter shook Trish from the other side of the couch. Revulsion brought her back to herself. She tried to smile but her face was more like the grimace of someone trying not to vomit. "I think I better go lie down."

As she climbed the stairs, Trish saw Deidre climb into Tony's lap, facing him, her chin tucked so she could peer out at him from under her eyelashes.

One afternoon after they'd had sex in the hotel, Trish told Luca about overhearing her mother's baby voice with her father. They had showered and were sitting in the suite's living room having coffee. She sat on Luca and did her best imitation, showing him the head tilt and the hair twirling.

"It's mystifying." Trish shook her head.

"It's just their thing." Luca slurped his coffee.

"You're saying this is how she pleases her man?"

Luca swallowed and raised his mug in consideration. "Maybe."

Trish inhaled deeply and told him about the time after her high school graduation, when she'd walked in on her parents from the kitchen.

"Definitely his thing," Luca confirmed.

"Gross. Why would a person demean themselves like that for the sake of a man?" An agitation set itself up in Trish's sternum.

"Have you known a lot of women?" Luca squinted at her.

"Of course."

"Cuz they're not all hell-bent on discovering the secrets of the universe."

"Girls are told from a very young age that math and science are for boys. It's a cultural problem. Women are not stupid, Luca." Now Trish was angry.

Luca's eyes met hers above his mug. "Smart enough to know when their men like little girls."

When Trish came into the kitchen for dinner, her parents were already eating. Her father looked up from his plate, saw the head, and gave a sharp laugh through his nose.

Trish put it down on the counter and, without planning to, said, "I've been remembering all these recurring nightmares I had as a kid."

"Oh yes, I heard about this," Deidre said to Tony. "She had a terrifying childhood, apparently."

Tony gave a small derisive laugh as he chewed. "I'll tell you what the nightmare is." He pointed with his fork to the head.

Somehow, at the thin end of Trish's patience was courage. "I didn't say I was dreaming. I said I was remembering."

Deidre put her fork down and turned to Trish. "You think you're so smart. You think you're so much smarter than everyone else. But you're not. Look where your smarts have gotten you." She nodded toward the head.

Hollow, Trish left the head on the counter and took her seat at the table. Coming here had been a mistake. She picked up her cutlery. "It smells good," she told her mother and cut into the meat on her plate.

"You might like to remember that you slept your way into your current position."

"What are you talking about?"

"Well, you did. You slept your way into university in the first place and then you slept with that Italian professor to get your current position."

Tony gave Deidre a questioning look.

"At least she had the taste to find an Italian man," Deidre told Tony.

He snorted his appreciation.

"I met Luca in my current position! He's a colleague. He didn't get me the position."

"Well, your little affair coincided just nicely with your tenure application."

"Luca has nothing to do with my tenure application. I'm a year out from submitting it and we just broke up! Besides, he studies algebra and I study geometry. You don't know what you're talking about. You paint hotel landscapes. You cannot talk to me about tenure applications!"

The head was crying on the counter now.

"And I did not have sex with Mr. Rose!" Trish shook her head. "For fuck's sake."

"Hey!" Tony bellowed from across the table, pointing his steak knife at her. "You do not talk to your mother that way."

"And besides, even if I had, I was a child. I needed protection, not shame."

"Well, you have feminism to protect you from your bad behaviour now."

Trish pushed away from the table, palmed the head like a baseball and carried it to her room while it screamed into her palm.

CHAPTER TEN

The next morning, Trish stood at the far end of the tub from the shower and wondered how her parents lived like this. The shower head was caked with lime and the spray was chaotic, with streams shooting off in all directions, some only mist, some sharp needles.

Scene of the crime echoed through her head.

Stupid mind. She shimmied past the spray to the shower head and scraped away some of the crust with her fingernails. The effort made no difference. She arched her back to keep away from the needles of spray, her breasts were cold in the air. Then, another childhood dream; later than the troll, around the time of the witch. In this dream, a superman costume emerged from the closet at the end of her bed. Only the costume. There was no head and there was no body inside the suit. In a kind of herky-jerky imitation of a walk, it floated out of the closet and through the air toward Trish as she lay frozen. Then the thing would slowly press itself over her, covering, one at a time, her feet, calves, thighs, hips, belly, and chest. The thing was so cold it burned. It left Trish's head free, and she took small sips of air so as not to disturb the thing as it pressed itself to her. In the mornings, she would remember the costume coming at her from the closet. But she never remembered how the dream ended.

During that time, Trish moved through the world as though it was a place of malevolent trolls, tickling witches, and headless supermen. During her waking hours, she tried to find the explanations for these aspects of the world. She searched down alleys for portals and set up shrines behind the garden shed. When a boy bullied her at the playground, spitting on the ground and forcing her to try to pick it up. Trish presumed it was some message from this dark side, a missive of shadows. Reality ran in dark layers.

And she was stupid enough to forget.

Back in her room, her phone rang as she got dressed. It was Jess. "You haven't answered any of my texts."

It seemed strange to think that only a few days ago, Trish was someone who had anything to communicate by text.

"Why won't you tell me what's going on?"

Trish held the phone and grew hot. If she spoke she would cry, so she shook her head into the phone.

"Are your parents helping, at least?"

A gasp of air escaped and released the flood of tears. "I just keep getting it wrong."

Poor Jess listening to all Trish's snot. "Trish, it's not the movies. Your parents are not… look, they're your family, so you love them, but I don't know if… if they have what you need right now."

Trish nodded and sniffed hard into the phone. "Sorry."

"For what?"

When Jess and Trish graduated, the Washingtons and Deidre came for the ceremony. Trish lied to her mother and said she could only get one ticket for a family member to the graduation and moved quickly to talk about how exciting the trip would be and what fun it would be for Deidre to meet the Washingtons, which was a mistake, of course. How could both of Jess's parents come if they were only allowed one ticket to graduation? But Deidre had only expressed excitement and enthusiasm for the trip. After the ceremony, they all went out for dinner at a fancy Italian restaurant. At dinner Mr. Washington asked after Tony, and Deidre made the excuse that he had to work.

"We aren't all blessed with the gifts that let us make our own schedule!" She was bragging about her art, but it sounded like she thought the Washingtons didn't understand the common man. Mr. Washington, who often worked fourteen-hour days, and whose wife was on call ten days of each month, raised a glass.

"Gratitude is indeed the path to a full heart."

At dinner Trish was happy. But she was nervous about the conversation because she was sure that if she opened her mouth, food would fall out, and everyone would see and then have to pretend they had not. Even when she managed to swallow, she would glance down at her new white blouse to be sure she hadn't dripped sauce. She imagined Dr. Washington watching the sauce fall from her fork. She just wanted to not disgust her dinner mates.

Over dessert and coffee, Mr. Washington made a toast. "To our daughter, Jessica, the light of our lives, and her lovely friend, Trish. You've both accomplished so much. And we're all very proud of you."

Trish was at a loss for how to respond to such an expression of affection from someone she so admired, and she felt guilty for having interfered with Jessica's toast from her father. She smiled uncomfortably into her apple crumble.

"Jessica probably didn't even have to sleep with her high school math teacher to get here," Deidre dispersed the warm feeling from the table.

Trish's heart clenched and her cheeks burned. She was sure there was ice cream on her chin, and rubbed at it hard.

"Mum!"

"Oh, sorry. I didn't even realize how insulting that would be to Jessica. I'm very sorry." Deidre reached out a hand to Dr. Washington and gazed mournfully down the table to Mr. Washington.

Jessica's mother ignored Deidre's hand on top of her own and shook her head sharply. "That's not… What do you mean?"

Trish could barely breathe.

"Oh, well," Deidre, clearly relieved that she had not insulted her new friends, waved a hand at Trish as though she was a fly on the table. "Trish made sure that her high school math teacher took a special interest in her, if you take my meaning." She panned the table with her laughter to be sure that everyone knew how funny it was that Trish had not legitimately earned her place in university. "But, you know, I always told her to use all her God-given gifts to make it in the world."

Mr. Washington was frozen, his coffee en route to his mouth, his neck craning and lips pursed in anticipation of the drink. Dr. Washington put her dessert spoon down quietly beside her bowl and leaned forward, the insides of her wrists resting against the table.

Trish sat devastated that her image had been ruined in front of the Washingtons, that they had been initiated into the second aspect of her dual-truth reality. She was furious with herself for imagining she could ever move through the world as though it didn't exist. Trish loved Jessica and felt lucky beyond her wildest dreams to get to know the Washingtons. Why had she pretended that was real? Now they were all gone, off to that other reality.

"Trish," Dr. Washington continued to ignore Deidre. "What happened?"

"To her?" Deidre's voice was shrill with the determination to laugh. "She got herself into university. I imagine that recommendation letter was quite effusive."

Dr. Washington closed her eyes against Deidre, and then looked at Trish.

"Nothing," Trish's voice cracked. "Nothing happened."

"Because if something happened, it was not your fault, and you were not responsible. You were a child."

"No, nothing." She met Dr. Washington's gaze. "Nothing happened. My parents… it's just this running joke."

Mr. Washington freed himself, sipped his coffee and cleared his throat. His cup clanked loudly in the saucer when he put it down.

Trish turned to Deidre and, with the solidity of the Washingtons in her heart, said, "Nothing untoward ever happened with Mr. Rose."

Deidre's aspect was solemn. "Well, why didn't you say so?"

Trish imagined the top of her skull as a pond filled with electric eels, fighting each other. She saw Jessica glance, wide-eyed, at her father.

"It's quite natural for children to feel unable to contradict their parents," Dr. Washington finally spoke to Deidre.

"Apparently so," Deidre raised her hands in an expression of confusion.

Later, in the restroom, Trish cried and told Jess that having that conversation was the first time she truly believed anyone thought she had legitimately earned her place at university.

"Oh god, of course you did!"

Jessica hugged her hard and swayed back and forth.

"You're the smartest person I know."

Trish threw the phone into her pack. How was the head? It wasn't crying, so it was probably fine, but it was worth checking. She presumed the quiet meant Deidre had given it the facecloth to suckle and she wondered how that had gone for her.

When Trish came into the kitchen, the head was not on the counter where she'd left it. Instead, Deidre's good crafting scissors sat alone and open on the granite. Deidre was at the sink staring out of the window. Trish could hear the head crying now. It was very quiet.

"Hey. Where's the head?"

Trish tracked back to check the living room. The sound of the cry faded as she moved to the front of the house. When she returned to the kitchen, she heard the head again. But it was quiet. Deidre still stared out of the kitchen window.

"Mum. Where's the head?"

"Oh Trish," she tsk'ed. "I did you a favour."

"What are you talking about? Where's the head?"

"I didn't think you'd be down so soon."

"Your shower sucks. Where's the head?"

Deidre did not move away from the sink but looked down into it. The garbage.

"What have you done?!"

Would Trish have the will to push her away from the cupboard door? But Deidre moved as she approached. She opened the door and the head's cries were louder but still muffled. She pulled on the garbage can. It was full of paper towels. Trish tossed aside handfuls of them and found the head, wrapped in paper towel, sitting on a bed of banana peels, used tissue, chewed gum and soft plastic wrap. Its face was cut deeply on the right-hand side, from the bottom of its eye socket all the way down to its jawbone.

"Ooooh. God. Are you okay?" Trish mewled. "I'm sorry, I'm sorry, I'm sorry. Sh. Sh. Sh. We'll get you fixed up. Don't worry. Sh. Sh. Sh."

She held paper towel to the edge of the bleeding wound. Fibres from the paper towel threatened to get into the wound itself. How was she going to deal with this? It's not like she could take it to the hospital for stitches. "What the hell?" she roared at her mother.

"Trish, stop it." Deidre grabbed Trish's wrist and shook her hand so that she might drop the head.

Trish tightened her grip and resisted the urge to pull away. She did not want the head to fly across the room.

Finally, Deidre stopped shaking and just held Trish's arm. Her other hand flew up and she slapped Trish hard across the face. Even as the world sang, Trish thought, *the same side she cut on the head.* "Enough!" Deidre let go of her wrist and Trish fled with the head up the stairs and locked herself in the bathroom.

Her right cheek flamed but she needed to deal with the head's wound. Her idea was to hold the cut closed with Band-Aids. The tiny ones weren't strong enough to hold the two sides together. Why is there never enough glue on those things? And the normal-sized Band-Aids went all the way from the head's tiny hairs to its nose. She cut two Band-Aids short with nail clippers and secured the cut together like that.

"Does that feel better?" she asked. "I'm sorry that happened."

She ran a hand under the cold water tap and held it to her stinging cheek. It felt good but the heat sprang back as soon as she took her hand away. As she thought about what to do, she cooled her cheek again. Her return flight wasn't until tomorrow. Go to the airport and change flights. Take one today. But security had been a nightmare. And now the head was bleeding. Drive. Keep the rental, and just drive it back to Cascadia. Once she struck upon the idea, relief flooded through her. There would be a return fee. She dithered. But thinking about security at the airport filled her with dread. Pay the fee.

Deidre was in the kitchen, sitting at the table, her hands empty in front of her.

Trish stood in the doorway across from her. "What were you thinking?"

Deidre just stared into the middle distance.

"Mum!"

Deidre did not look at her. "I never told you, but I had an abortion when I was seventeen."

"What?"

"Patty took me. She drove me in her green Pinto. Remember that thing? On the way there, the smell of cigarettes in the ashtray made me queasy. But then on the way back it didn't bother me at all."

Trish stroked the head's uninjured cheek with the pad of her thumb. "Who was the father?"

"A boy I met at a party. He never called again after that one night. I was genuinely surprised. He said such kind things to me. Anyway, Patty drove, and she came in with me and held my hand and then she was there in the waiting room when I came out. It's a physically hollow feeling, which I wasn't expecting. Like when you're dieting, and hunger feels good. Except more noticeable because it doesn't grow, like hunger. It's a sudden emptiness. On the way home we stopped at the liquor store. We wanted to get drunk. And that's where I met your father. He was working at the cash register. He was such a charmer. Joked with us when we came in and then so brave to just ask for my number when we brought our beer to the counter."

Trish had known her parents met at a liquor store. "You met him the same day you had an abortion?"

Deidre gave a small snort of nodding laughter. "Patty was so encouraging. She was so happy for me that your father was interested. When we got back in the car she said, 'See, you're going to be fine.'" She frowned at the table. "You know, if I'm honest about it, I had a little niggle of surprise that she was happy and not jealous. And I was so proud of myself for having such a great friend and now maybe a man. I felt so grown up. But then in the end, they did have an affair. When you were a baby."

"What? Are you serious?"

"Yes. Your father had an affair with Patty."

"God. Gross. Uuuuggh." Trish put the head down on the counter and buried her face in her hands.

"I was so angry. I didn't want you to have her name anymore, but I didn't want to confuse you. I didn't know then how resilient children are."

The head whimpered on the counter, and Trish scooped it up.

"Your father thinks we ought to take you to the hospital."

Suddenly Trish was exhausted. The head, warm in her hand, clicked its little tongue. "No."

"I told him you'd say that."

"I'm leaving now."

Deidre nodded but didn't move. Trish felt bad leaving her like that.

"I have to go now."

Deidre followed Trish out to the car and stood on the sidewalk as she loaded her suitcase into the back. She held her arms open, and they hugged. Trish had never felt so alone. She drove through town, and stopped at a McDonald's for coffee before getting on the highway. As she sat in the car, she texted Jess.

> You were right. It was a mistake to come here. I'm going home.
> I'm driving.
> I can't face the airport.

What happened?
Why don't you drive here. Come here.

> No. There's too much going on.
> I need to get back to Cascadia.

What happened?

> It's too complicated.
> But my mother told me my dad cheated on her with her friend Patty.
> The one she named me after.

Patty?

> Patricia.

Oh Jesus. Right. Are you sure you don't want to come here? There's a new doughnut place.

> You are really excited about this doughnut place.
> I just need to be alone.

Okay. Call me when
you get there.

It'll be the middle of the night.

Okay. Call me in the
morning, please.
Promise?

Promise.

Trish kept the head in her lap as she drove. At times it was overwhelming to have its weight on her legs, but at least it didn't cry. When she sang, it closed its eyes, which made Trish laugh. No one had ever complimented her singing.

She needed to decide what to do. She could not be alone like this anymore. Everyone told her she had to give this thing up. That she could not take care of it. No one wanted to acknowledge it. No one wanted it in the world. But it felt so urgently important to Trish. This holy terror had set off a string of events that had unravelled her life. But how? She'd found this thing and remembered some dreams. Only Trish could consider memories of dreams the unravelling of a life.

But she saw the pattern. Each time she got into the shower after the head, she remembered a dream. The head had arrived while she was in the shower. Now that she had made the connection, she felt a resonance in the pattern. Had the head's appearance set up the pattern or was the head of a kind with the memories? The head was a physical presence, not a memory. But mathematically, time was no different from the other dimensions. The head and the dreams were of a kind. They were her proofs.

CHAPTER ELEVEN

As she drove into the foothills, one or two drops of rain fell onto the windshield. She still had half a tank of gas, but she decided to fill up before starting into the mountains, just to be safe. Rain in the plains would be snow higher up. She stopped for gas in a little ski town called Bracken which she had visited a couple of times as a child but which was entirely unfamiliar to her now. As she stood listening to the pump's whirr and click, it began to rain in earnest and Trish heard herself think, *scene of the crime*. The nozzle popped shut and she walked to the store to pay.

Trish glanced up at the bank of screens behind the cashier's head. A woman with her back to the camera was filling her tank with the kind of grace, calm, and composure that, only three or four days ago, Trish had decided she would embody. She had not even thought about that promise since the head's arrival—abandoned it entirely. So typical, letting herself be overwhelmed by reality.

The woman on the camera smoothly removed the gas nozzle from her car and flipped the door of the tank shut with a flick of her wrist. She turned to come into the store with a strength, solidity, assuredness that Trish could only envy. Trish looked out the door to watch the woman come in. But there was no one coming. Was this like the head's sudden appearance? Trish looked quickly back to the screens and that's when she saw the woman's face. It was her. The video was delayed.

Outside the store, Trish stood between bundles of firewood wrapped in plastic, and a pallet full of windshield washer fluid and dialed Jess's number.

"Can I still come?"

"That would be amazing."

"Don't be too sure," Trish sniffed and wiped her nose. "I'm not at my best."

"That's why I want you."

"I won't be there until tomorrow. I'm going to drive up through the mountains—take my time."

Trish drove north through the mountains, taking the head with her when she stopped to marvel at the views, or sit and eat a sandwich, drink her coffee. The shapes around her inspired her and she thought through some problems she'd been working on, and Brandon's manifolds. She stroked the head's little cheeks and murmured to it about the beauty around them and her ideas. But she did not think about the math department.

At Mount Robinson, where she would need to turn east for Jess, Trish parked and carried the head as she hiked up a steep rise to Dog Sled falls. The water, placid and jade green just fifty feet upstream roared white over the falls before continuing west in a white and emerald rush to the ocean. Trish knew she was right—the head had come to her, unbidden. Still, she had never wanted the head to suffer. And it did not want for her to suffer. She had comforted it, thought of its wellbeing, and in so doing, taken care of herself, considered her own wellbeing. That was all it had intended: to change her perspective. She did not feel bad for the head. The head did not need her. And Trish did not need the head. She would miss its soft warmth. But a proof was the ground from which to grow, to unfold. Trish would flourish from her proof. She did not need to carry it.

She drew back her arm and hurled the head as hard as she could into the chop. It popped up once and was gone, pulled under and swept along in the glacial water. Trish sank onto her knees, truly empty. Deep, heavy sadness sat on her shoulders, and she cried.

The water splashed and she listened. Funny how she could hear a higher-pitched splash within the broad roar of the falls. She opened her eyes and watched the water dance over the falls. And then she stood. She wanted to get to Jess by nightfall.

ACKNOWLEDGEMENTS

It's well-nigh impossible to express my gratitude and appreciation for all the people who were critical to this book, which was first the thesis for my MFA.

Thanks first to the folks at Enfield and Wizenty who wanted to publish the book so fast that I'm still not sure it's true. Keith's cool never flagged, which made it all doable.

Maureen Medved encouraged me to develop my short story assignment for her class into a longer work. Her faith in the story and my work was terrifying and thrilling.

It's been my tremendous good fortune to work with John Vigna and learn from his gracious approach to fiction, and teaching, and teaching fiction. Thank you for all of it.

Bronwen Tate taught me how to take my craft seriously, a gift that makes much possible. Thanks, too, for supervising the thesis with patience and good humour.

I knew I needed Tonya Lailey as a friend about six weeks into the MFA. And I was right. I do need you! I can't even say. Thank you for everything, including the countless drafts.

Kimberley Orton, your love gives me one of my favourite feelings—that I'm getting away with something. Such windfall.

Erin McGregor's eyes and wit are keen in equal measure. Thank you for pointing out the ending of the book to me. Edmonton misses you.

And of course the Bees and beyond: Emily Cann, Jason Emde, Theresa Eleanore Fuller, Jaymie Heilman, Shelley Kawaja, Barbara Bruhin Kenney, Alison Newall, Leslie Palleson, Andrea Scott and my mama, Barbara Smith. This book would never have been written if I hadn't been doubled over in laughter half the time.

Finally, thanks to Emmett. When I started this project you were the best little boy in the world, and now you're the best young man in the world, and I have been the luckiest mum the whole time.